SINGING LEAD

Ben Harvey had dedicated his life to fighting the forces of evil. That's why he had joined the Texas Rangers in the first place. Perhaps the most dangerous job he'd tackled was the cleaning up of the Stangle gang. By matching cunning with cunning he was able to get himself accepted as a member of the owlhoot band—but having joined the lion in his mountain den he had still to beard him. If he succeeded in his mission, the secret of a gold mine would remain with its rightful owner and Jed Stangle would end up in the noose of a rawhide rope. If he failed—a .45 slug would send him quickly on a single journey to Boothill!

NAT LAZENBY

SINGING LEAD

Complete and Unabridged

LINFORD
Leicester

First Linford Edition
published March 1989

Copyright © 1949 by Norman Lazenby

British Library CIP Data

Lazenby, Nat
    Singing lead.—Large print ed.—
Linford western library
I. Title
823'.914[F]

ISBN 0-7089-6678-0

Published by
F. A. Thorpe (Publishing) Ltd.
Anstey, Leicestershire
Set by Rowland Phototypesetting Ltd.
Bury St. Edmunds, Suffolk
Printed and bound in Great Britain by
T. J. Press (Padstow) Ltd., Padstow, Cornwall

1

Renegade Ranger

BEN HARVEY raced his bay horse over the grassy ridge at a full lope. He was three-quarters of a mile ahead of the sheriff and his posse. The horse was sweating, but Ben wanted grimly to keep that lead.

Trees lining Palermo Creek afforded him plenty of cover. The posse could not see him now. He turned the bay into the creek and waded him upstream.

He went on for fully half a mile. Then, jerking at the reins, he scrambled the horse out of the creek and rode hell-for-leather back into the hills.

Meanwhile the posse rode across the prairie, missed the creek and dashed into the sun-baked settlement of Palermo, a crude collection of adobe huts and tin shacks.

A dozen of the posse jumped from their horses, scattered, and entered the rough stores that lined the main street. Grimly nestling in their arms they carried rifles. Their boots scraped and thumped on the boards.

The sheriff, Hoot Bainter, burst into the Palermo Saloon. His eyes were grim, his moustache bristled. He thought the saloon the best place for the sheriff of the posse to operate in.

"You!" He addressed the sallow-faced bartender with the gold teeth. "Where did that hombre go?"

The bartender polished a glass leisurely.

"What hombre, Sheriff?"

"That lean galoot with the black hat and green shirt?"

"I didn't see him."

Sheriff Bainter glared round the saloon at the characters that lounged there.

"Any of you see that hombre ride in?"

Some of the men shrugged, others turned their backs deliberately. The sheriff made a rumbling sound in his throat.

"You hombres wouldn't be hidin' him, would yuh?"

"We ain't hidin' nobody," said the bartender.

"Lissen, hidin' men is the only durned business you got in Palermo," snarled Sheriff

Bainter. "If you ain't hidin' him, somebody is. That hombre headed thisaway."

"Maybe you got things all wrong," said the bartender, coolly.

"I got things right!" bawled the sheriff. He hitched up his cartridge belt. "Some day I'm going to catch you hombres hoppin' and I'll burn this saloon to the ground. There ain't an honest man in the goldarned place."

The bartender grinned, showing his bad teeth.

"You must want that feller bad."

"That galoot just walked down Toughgrass City. He robbed two places and rode out. One man ain't going to live. Cussedest nerve I ever saw!"

"Who is this hombre?" asked the bartender, curiously.

"Name o' Ben Harvey!" snapped the sheriff. "We'll get our hands on him an' we'll nail his hide to a barn door!"

The bartender held his glass to the light and polished it a bit more.

"If I see the jigger, I'll let yuh know, Sheriff."

Bainter moved away in disgust.

"Yeah? When anybody in Palermo turns in a renegade, you'll all be drinking orange juice!"

Sheriff Bainter turned to his men behind him.

"Right, fellers. Go through this rathole. And if yuh see Harvey shoot first and ask yuh questions later. He oughta be in this town somewheres—he made fer here."

Meanwhile, Ben Harvey worked his way through the scrub timber, following a deer trail towards higher ground. He went past three massive junipers standing beside a rocky outcrop, and, dismounting, untied a flour sack from his saddle. He took out a mixed collection of silver and paper money and put it into his pockets. Then he buried the sack among the rocks and dirt.

He paused for a moment to make himself a cigarette, and smiled with recollections of the fast ride out of Toughgrass.

He wondered how Sheriff Bainter was making out in Palermo.

According to the plan, Sheriff Bainter would be spreading the word in Palermo. The sheriff would lay it on. That was part of the plan. The word would soon get around that a gunman

4

named Ben Harvey was wanted for robberies in Toughgrass.

Ben lit his cigarette with a sulphur match and drew on it with some satisfaction. All he had to do now was contact Jed Stangle's gang.

And when he was accepted as part of the gang he would have to find a way to turn them in— dead or alive.

Ben flicked his cigarette thoughtfully. He had a tough assignment, even for a special man of the famed Texas Rangers. In his broad leather belt, in a specially concealed pocket, was his badge. No one would find the gleaming silver star set on a silver circle which was the feared and honoured badge of the Rangers.

Ben Harvey was a big man, but he had a suggestion of litheness in his every movement. His face was brown, lean and thoughtful, but there were lines that suggested he could grin quickly, and his steady grey eyes and dark crisp hair completed his rugged handsomeness. In his role of gunman he wore two Colts, lying low on his lean thighs.

Back at Headquarters, Captain MacAdam had been known to say of Harvey: "He's as stubborn as a mule, quick as a mountain cat and the match of any Texan with a Colt. I like him."

This quest for Jed Stangle was no ordinary job. In the vast country which was Texas there were many bands of desperadoes. Jed Stangle and his men had been just one more mob until recently. Then, two weeks ago, Jed had kidnapped old Tom Wilson.

Wilson was a very special character in the district, he owned a large ranch and was making it pay. But only a few years ago he had no money. Then he had found his mine out in the labyrinthine maze of unmapped canyons that marks the edge of the Guadalupe mountains in a wild section of the Lone Star State. Tom Wilson had found an incredibly rich strike of gold—raked the nuggets in with a shovel as he often said. He made frequent trips into the desolate country, always returning with a poke full of nuggets. So rich was his find, he never bothered with dust or fine stuff.

But Old Tom never registered his claim and he never told anyone the location of the bonanza deposit. He just made his periodic trips into the mountains, returning to the frontier town of Odessa and banking his gold. Tom did not trust anyone. For long years he had spent his time in the desert country seeking gold, and now he had found it he intended to keep others out.

And then he had bought the Flying T spread down near Toughgrass, about five miles from Palermo. He had married a widow, Mary Harper, with a grown-up daughter named Linda, and had settled down on his ranch, forgetting the bonanza in the dangerous and desolate wilderness of the Guadalupe mountains. For Tom now had enough for his needs.

And then two weeks ago, Jed Stangle had kidnapped Tom Wilson. Tom had just disappeared, and the rumours had gone round the town. Somehow or other everyone knew that Stangle was after the location of the gold mine. He would make Tom Wilson speak.

So Captain MacAdam had sent Ben Harvey to Toughgrass. Ben had met up with the sheriff secretly and arranged the rumpus he had created in Toughgrass the following day.

For Ben's information was that Jed Stangle's gang was still hiding in the hills surrounding the lawless town of Palermo. Just where, no one knew for certain, and when any attempt was made by the sheriff of Toughgrass to ride a posse into the hills Jed simply shifted his gang temporarily.

The fact that Stangle was still in the hills above Palermo, meant that Old Tom Wilson had not spoken about his gold mine. It meant that Tom was holding out, somehow, under the pressure Stangle would be bound to bring to bear on him.

Tom Wilson had to be rescued and soon: those were Ben's orders. The kidnapping of Tom Wilson had become a matter of prestige. Stangle had to be beaten on this point.

Ben finished his cigarette and stowed away the paper and silver money in his pockets. This was money he was supposed to have stolen in Toughgrass. If he met up with Jed Stangle he would need to have all his details right.

One thing he was thankful for—he was unknown in these parts of Texas. He had worked in the east and was quite sure he'd be unrecognised in this western section of the state.

Ben started along the deer trail again, his bay picking a good path for such a heavy horse.

There was one thing which put him at a disadvantage: he did not know these hills round Palermo. But he was an expert at trailcraft, and being a Texas Ranger meant he had adaptability. He would learn this country quickly.

During his talk last night with Sheriff Bainter, he had gotten all the necessary facts that the other had in his possession. Ben knew that somewhere in these hills Stangle kept a hideout, but Jed and his men were often drinking in Palermo; the town was that sort of place. It was entirely lawless. Even the sheriff of Toughgrass avoided it.

Ben was figuring to meet up with Jed Stangle somehow. And Palermo was the place.

He went on for an hour along the trail and was climbing up past some buttes when a rider jogged suddenly from behind an outcrop of rock.

The stranger made no other move, but eyed Ben calmly. He was a lean, stringy Border character who wore two guns slung in shiny holsters. He had black, beady eyes that flicked unceasingly over Ben's horse, clothes and guns.

"Hyar, stranger!" he called. "You a long way outa Palermo."

Ben halted a few feet away from the man, wondering just how he had appeared so suddenly.

"I'm looking for a hombre," he replied. "You wouldn't know where I can find Jed Stangle, would yuh?"

The other shook his unshaven jaw and close-cropped head.

"That gent is mighty hard to find. Yuh might say he's partikler who he meets. Who are yuh, stranger? Ain't seen yuh in Palermo last time I was down there."

"Name is Ben Harvey," said Ben, shortly. "I'm looking for Stangle because I figured he might have a place for a hombre anxious to make himself scarce for a few weeks."

The other nodded, but his eyes were still wary.

"Happens I meet this Jed Stangle, I'll let him know," he said in deliberate tones.

And with those few words Ben Harvey knew there was no need to search much further. His message would reach Jed Stangle's ears pretty soon. Jed Stangle would be told that a gent wearing a black, rakish hat and a green shirt was looking for him and Stangle would want to find out something about him.

The stringy man kept his horse standing across the trail deliberately. It was a plain hint to Ben that he need go no further. It was a plain hint that solitary wandering hombres were not encouraged to ride along that trail.

"Reckon I'll be in Palermo for the next few

hours," drawled Ben. "Maybe I'll meet Jed Stangle there. Hope yuh remember the name is Ben Harvey, hombre!"

The other nodded. His eyes dropped again to Ben's two guns.

"I got a good memory. Happens I meet this Jed Stangle I'll let him know about yuh."

Ben turned his horse slowly and rode deliberately down the deer trail.

Ben rode down from the hills and entered Palermo as the ramshackle town sweltered in the evening sun.

In the few streets, deep in alkali, chickens and pigs rummaged, while back of the shacks Mexican and white children played and shouted.

Ben found a Chinese eat-house and he stopped to have some jerky meat, beans and gravy. There was one thing about the Chinks who were to be found everywhere—they knew how to dish the chow out.

From the restaurant he went along to the Palermo Saloon. He had it from Sheriff Bainter that the saloon was the focal point of the worst ruffians who used Palermo. Jed Stangle, when he got tired of the hills, often dropped into the

Palermo Saloon to drink and play cards. In Palermo he could enjoy these little amenities safe from the law, which was something he could not do in Toughgrass.

Ben ordered his liquor from the bartender with the gold teeth. He knew the bartender stared for a brief but decisive second at his green shirt and black hat. It was a good quality rigout. Ben knew Sheriff Bainter would have circulated his description thoroughly.

There was plenty of rotgut whiskey on the pine counter. Ben, who could drink anything, thought it was pretty bad.

"Bring me the best next time," he said coldly to the bartender, and he flipped a bill on the counter.

The bartender stared, showing his two gold teeth and his host of bad ones.

"Anything yuh say," he muttered.

He brought the drink. Ben gulped half of it and noted it was a sight better than the first.

"Sheriff Bainter of Toughgrass was lookin' for a feller in Palermo today," said the bartender carefully. "Said the hombre was wearing a black hat and a green shirt."

Ben grinned at the bartender.

"That so? I wonder why he didn't catch that hombre?"

The bartender grinned at Ben.

"Sure seemed mighty annoyed, that Sheriff. Said this hombre robbed some galoots in Toughgrass and got away with plenty."

Ben dropped his grin.

"Maybe he did an' maybe he didn't. Another drink, feller."

The bartender ceased to be confidential. Judging by the way he ducked for the bottle at the back of the counter, he did not like the sudden glint in Ben's eyes.

"I want a bed, feller," said Ben to the bartender.

"Sure, but yuh gotta sign a register." And the bartender grinned slyly. "That's what the law says."

"Can't say I noticed much law around here," drawled Ben.

And he wrote his name—Ben Harvey—in the register and put down his address as Tucson, Arizona.

"Yuh travelled a long way, mister," said the bartender.

"Yeah," said Ben. "The room, feller?"

Ben was shown to his room. It was a bare

place but the bed looked good. Ben thought he could use it. He had been up half the night talking plans with Sheriff Bainter.

"See to my hoss, will yuh?" he asked the bartender, and he peeled off a bill from the roll which he was supposed to have stolen. The bartender did not miss a thing.

"Shore will, mister. There's a livery next door."

Ben lay down on the bed when the man had gone. He lay with his hands under his head, thinking.

He dozed a little. He had figured he might see Jed Stangle in Palermo tonight if the other came into town. If he did not, he would have to get started on another plan to contact the outlaw.

A knock came on the door, and Ben sat bolt upright. The door opened and three men walked in. One was the Border ruffian whom he had encountered on the trail in the hills that afternoon. The other two Ben did not know.

But they were both big men, and they packed two guns. One man, big burly with a red moustache and a livid bullet scar across his cheek, was obviously Jed Stangle.

"Howdy, Harvey," said the man Ben had

14

met previously. "I've brought a few friends to see yuh."

Ben slid off the bed and stood upright. He grinned. The man had obviously got his name from the bartender downstairs. And, just as obviously, he'd have the whole story of the holdup in Toughgrass, the ride out with the posse after his tail.

2

Trip To Toughgrass

"I DIDN'T get yore names?" hinted Ben.

The Border man twisted his lips in a smile.

"Shore. Call me Jeff Muldoon. This is Rocky Creel." He indicated the huge, inscrutable man with the hard bony face. "And this is a gent yuh talked about wantin' tuh see this afternoon up on the trail. Jed Stangle."

Ben acknowledged the introductions.

"What yuh want to see me about?" queried Jed Stangle. There was no other expression in his blue eyes but cold calculating ruthlessness. He was looking at Ben as if to read his mind.

Ben took out the makings of a cigarette. He rolled the smoke slowly and talked slowly.

"I figured yuh were a man who did things in a big way. I'm a bit tired o' chicken-feed. I want to make me some dinero, so I reckon I got to make the right contacts."

16

Jed Stangle smoothed his bristly red moustache.

"I heard yuh got some dinero out o' Tough-grass today. Where is it?"

Ben unbuttoned his shirt, took out his roll from a pocket sewn inside. He flicked the roll, looked at Jed Stangle.

"That ain't exactly chicken-feed," growled the other. "Let me count it. If yuh aimin' to come in with us, yuh got tuh split half. That's the way we work."

"But I got this money on my own," protested Ben.

Jed Stangle shot the roll back at Ben.

"Hold it," he said. "We'll talk about it later. Where yuh come from?"

"I could say Tucson," said Ben. "But does it matter?"

"Sometimes. An' I like a hombre to answer me straight."

"Shore. Yuh get straight answers from me, Stangle."

"Is Harvey yore real name?"

Ben laughed. "It's real enough."

Stangle just stood and looked at him grimly. Rocky Creel sneered. "This hellion acts too independent, Stangle. I don't like him."

17

"Shut up. I wasn't talking to yuh," said Ben, without turning his head.

Rocky Creel bunched his fists and stepped closer to Ben. His bony face, although inscrutable and granite-like, showed his anger.

"Lissen, Harvey. I'm Jed Stangle's *segundo*. I don't like yuh. I don't like the way yuh talk. I aim tuh show Stangle yuh ain't fer us."

His fist shot out. Had it connected it might have laid Harvey out. But Ben was used to fighting men who gave every indication they intended to strike. He dodged the blow with a lithe swerve of his head, his feet never moved. He straightened in a split second and like lightning his fists bunched and rammed out. It was the classic one-two.

But when Ben's fist connected it seemed to strike iron-rock. Not for nothing had Rocky Creel got his name. His bony face was incredibly hard. In addition, the man had an iron frame and a good fourteen stone deadweight.

Dropping his fists, the outlaw lowered his head and rushed in with all pretence at fist fighting thrown away. But Ben met the lowered head with a quickly moved knee which came up under Creel's face.

18

As Rocky slithered backwards, his boots making rasping sounds on the bare boards out of the room, Ben came closer and with savage fists helped Creel on the way down.

But the blows did not keep him down. With a roar he clutched at the bed, heaved himself up, and shook his head to clear some blood from a cut over his eye. He rushed into Ben, caught hold of his arm and heaved him into the orbit of his grip. His arms went round Ben like the arms of a bear. The two men locked and Creel endeavoured to swing Ben off the floor and then crash him down. With Ben the lighter man by about a stone, it seemed he might manage it. Ben strained against the other's pressure, and for a time there was only the sound of their hard breathing in the room. Jeff Muldoon was grinning as if unconcerned about the outcome of the fight. Jed Stangle was watching closely, his hands on his hips.

Then Ben jerked, first back and then forward, as if changing his tactics. He caught Creel off balance for a brief second. It was the merest second of opportunity, and Ben's quickness helped him. His foot entwined with Creel's, and the man fell backwards. Then off balance, he was going down again.

He hit the floorboards with a thud that nearly dislocated the timbers of the ramshackle two-storey building. As he hit the floor, Ben got clear of him.

Creel dazedly tried to rise. Before he even sat up, Ben slammed a right and left into his face. Ben was not obeying any fancy fighting rules. He was out to beat Creel as Creel would try to smash him—and that was by any means in or out of the book.

Creel sank to the boards with a groan. He snarled something unintelligible to Jed Stangle. It seemed that Stangle understood for briefly he nodded to Ben a signal to quit fighting.

"Creel shouldn't bandy words if he can't back them up!" gasped Ben. "Now do I get in with yuh?"

Stangle nodded. He had not smiled once. It seemed he hardly ever smiled.

"Yuh'll do," he said. "Actions are better than words. Yuh can tell me any fancy tale about yuh name or where yuh come from, and it don't mean a thing. But I seen some action. Yuh look like yuh can handle men. Yuh can work with me an' Creel—an' if Creel can't handle men in future it will be too bad!"

"Good," grunted Ben. "I figured you'd see I can be useful."

Jed Stangle held out his hand.

"That dinero you made. I want half. I got expenses. And that's our rule—fifty-fifty with me. I get half, the boys get the other half shared out between them. Yuh actually gaining on this deal, Harvey."

Ben smiled slowly, flipped the roll and counted out half the value of the bills.

"Yuh make a hard bargain, Stangle," Ben grunted. "I figured this dinero might set me up. Shore hope I make contact with something big soon. I'd like tuh see some dividend from this little investment o' mine."

Jed Stangle pocketed the bills, and glanced significantly at Jeff Muldoon. The Border breed, who, judging by his name, was half-Irish and half-Mexican, grinned at Stangle.

"Yore a stranger around here," began Stangle, "or yuh'd know more about me. Ain't yuh heard anything about Tom Wilson?"

Ben looked surprised. He shot a brief glance at Rocky Creel who had sat on the bed, nursing his face, and shook his head.

"Nope. I can't say I heard of the hombre," said Ben. "Who is this Wilson? Yore pal?"

Stangle permitted a shadowy smile to cross his leathery face.

"He's a cussed old galoot who knows where there's more gold than a dozen men could rightly carry away in years," spat Jed Stangle. He suddenly looked savagely angry.

"Gold? Where? In Texas?" asked Ben, suddenly very interested.

"About two hundred miles from here, among the canyons at the foot of the Guadalupe mountains. But that's all I can get from that durned old fool."

"Yuh mean yuh got this galoot?" queried Ben.

He took out the "makings" again, looking up at Stangle as if very interested.

"Shore; we got him up in my hideout," rapped Stangle. "Every hombre in Toughgrass and Palermo knows that."

Rocky Creel lifted his head sullenly.

"Shore. How come yuh don't know that, Harvey?"

"I told yuh I travelled a long way. Just rode into Toughgrass today. I've still got to figure out this country."

"Yuh're a fast worker," sneered Creel. "Yuh ride into a town and pull a holdup. How come yuh knew about Jed Stangle if yuh a stranger to these parts?"

"I rode down the Chisholm Trail with a breed who shore talked about yuh, Stangle. We parted before we hit the town."

"What was the breed like?" Jed Stangle shot the question.

"He was a battle-scarred hombre," retorted Ben quickly. "He had a milky right eye and two fingers missin'. Said he wasn't liked in Toughgrass, an' so he didn't ride in."

Stangle exchanged glances with Jeff Muldoon. Rocky Creel tightened his sullen mouth.

"That was Jose Carrillo," commented Stangle. "I didn't know that breed was outa jail. He used to work fer me."

Ben Harvey kept to himself the knowledge that Jose Carrillo was still in Tuma County Jail. It was a bit of information he had got from Sheriff Bainter. But Jose Carillo would not be out for some time, and it would be a good idea from now on if no one knew what had happened to the breed.

"Yuh'll do, Harvey," said Stangle. "Get yoreself yore beauty sleep and be up that deer trail tomorrer. Yuh'll meet Muldoon an' he'll bring yuh the rest o' the way."

The three men tramped out, and Ben sat on the bed and thought, smilingly.

Ben thought it would be a good idea if he went over to Toughgrass to see Sheriff Bainter. After tomorrow he might not be able to contact the sheriff easily.

He took off his green shirt, noting that it had been torn during the fight. He rummaged in the small bag he had brought upstairs. He got out a new shirt. It was red. He also had a spare hat —a grey sombrero. His pants were dark brown material and no different from hundreds of others.

He quickly changed into the fresh clothes, placed a chair against the door, making sure it was well jammed. Then he tied his boots round his neck and, in stocking feet, went to the window. He had noted it led to a sloping roof that finished with a gutter with about a seven foot drop to the ground. He could get out easily. The yard was dark and no one ever came round the back of the place. He could get away in the gloom, and return just as easily.

Ben went slithering down the small roof, hit

the gutter and then dropped lightly to the ground. He quickly pushed his feet into his boots. He walked quickly away from the place, down the back streets of Palermo. Once or twice a man passed him in the gloom, but as there was no moon Ben was sure he could not be recognised.

He came to a corral where a dozen unsaddled horses stood and cropped the thin grass. The horses probably belonged to some ranny in Palermo who dealt in horses. Pausing for a second, he knew that there was only one way.

He would have to borrow one!

Ben climbed into the corral, chose his horse quickly. It was a stocky little pinto. He could ride the animal nicely without a saddle—for a few miles anyway.

Ben spent two minutes fondling the pinto's head and ears. He figured it was a good idea to make a friend of the animal, for horses were creatures that liked human friends.

Finally he led the pinto out of the corral, replaced the rail and climbed to the horse's back. He gave the cayuse a slap and hugged the animal's neck, lying low, as the sturdy horse sprinted out of Palermo.

The five miles to Toughgrass were nothing

under the pinto's flying hoofs, and soon Ben had to think of tethering the cayuse in some hidden place out of the town.

He had not been seen leaving Palermo, and he did not intend to be seen entering Toughgrass. The sheriff's office lay on a corner of the block, away from the saloons and their lights. In addition, Ben knew there was a back entrance to the sheriff's office, and he had arranged with Hoot Bainter to adopt a certain knock as a signal of his presence.

Ben found a clump of cottonwoods in which he could hide his borrowed cayuse. He thought it would not be found, for no one would be out of town at night except those who were travelling and they would stick to the trail.

He came in on foot, wary and keeping to the shadowy back alleys and rough paths, through the houses and stores. It was not difficult to avoid other people, though now and then a man glanced curiously as Ben went by. But it was just the involuntary glance of one passerby to another. Ben reached the rough yard behind the sheriff's office. It was partly brick-built, with a strong lock-up with barred windows.

Ben halted outside the back door which led to the sheriff's living quarters. A family man was Sheriff Bainter, and he would be at home. Ben could see light from the living-room window. The saloons were not for Hoot Bainter these days.

He was just about to knock with his pre-arranged tat-tat when a commotion of shouts and thundering hoofs sprang up at the front of the sheriff's office. It could be Hoot Bainter, coming to investigate, figured Ben.

Ben instinctively sidled round to the front, keeping all the time in the shadows. He saw Sheriff Bainter's agressive form as he shouted back to a rider. A yellow shaft of light fell on the rider, showing his sweating horse as it snorted and blowed.

"Jed Stangle's men raided the Flying T," shouted the rider. "Came in with their durned hoglegs shootin' the ground 'neath our feet! Bust inter the ranch-house and whisked offen Miss Linda quicker than buzzard divin' on a dead hoss."

"They got her?" bawled Sheriff Bainter, incredulously.

"Sure, an' us rannies couldn't do a durn thing. Half the galoots are in town tonight spending their pay. Reckon—"

"Which trail did them hellions take?" roared Hoot Bainter.

The rider spat dust out of his mouth.

"Don't rightly know. They jest got swallered up in the night. Gone into the hills, I reckon."

"Doggone that skunk!" snapped the sheriff. He wheeled for the livery stable adjacent to the office. "What sorta trick is he up to now? What's he want Miss Linda for? He's got her old man. Now the girl! I gotta get a posse. Durn his hide!"

Ben heard everything and the meaning of Jed Stangle's move was quite clear to him. Old Tom Wilson was proving stern material and would probably die sooner than let a ruffian like Stangle horn in on his gold mine in the Guadalupes. But Stangle could not afford to let Tom Wilson die, and he probably could not afford to torture him beyond a safety point. Tom Wilson had obviously stuck it to this point and beyond. But if Tom Wilson cared for his step-daughter—and from all accounts he did quite a lot—then he would hate to see her suffer.

Obviously the outlaw wanted to use the girl as a lever to make Tom Wilson talk. And Ben

Harvey thought he knew where Jed Stangle's men would be heading with the girl.

Hoot Bainter was in the livery feverishly getting hold of his horse when Ben stopped in unknown to the rider outside. He came as silently as an Indian tracker up to the sheriff, and grinned as he spoke unexpectedly.

"Howdy—Sheriff!"

Sheriff Bainter's boots scraped as he wheeled swiftly. For a heavy-set man of forty-two, Hoot Bainter could move quickly.

"Tarnation! What the hell yuh doin' here? If the posse that was after yuh today sees yuh—"

"They haven't seen me," interrupted Ben. "Lissen, Hoot, I've contacted Stangle. Taken the first step to gettin' that hellion to a necktie party. Tell yuh more later. I heard the rider telling yuh about Linda Harper. I figure Stangle or his men took the girl to a hideout above the hills around Palermo. I reckon I know the trail —or part o' it. Let's get goin'. You an' me. Forget about a posse. Two men can work better in them hills. I see yuh got two hosses here."

"Sure. Yuh welcome to one. But if any hombre sees us together—"

"Meet me beside that clump o' cottonwoods

29

near the creek," rapped Ben. "With two hosses. Tell yuh rider yuh got ideas about contacting Stangle. Tell him anything. Get rid o' him somehow. The less they know about me the better."

Hoot Bainter nodded. He had quickly caught on to the plan. It was as good as anything, because a posse took time to round up, and in any case the kidnappers had a good head start. It was always the same. The law was always last to move.

Ben slipped away out of a back entrance to the livery, and made his way quickly through the unlighted parts of the town. Once clear of the buildings, he broke into a run and reached the cottonwoods just as Sheriff Bainter rode up on a bay mare, leading a bronc.

Ben let loose the pinto, slapped its flank. It ran off, and he figured it would head for the corral at Palermo. Some hombre, who was probably not too law-abiding, would wonder how the pinto had got out of the corral!

In a second he climbed to the saddled dun-coloured bronc. Spurring the horse to its full extent, he and the sheriff pounded along the trail leading to Palermo.

3

Coyotes' Camp

BEFORE they breasted a grassy ridge that led to Palermo Creek, up which he had waded his horse a few hours ago, Ben spotted the little used path which he guessed cut short the ride to the hilly deer trails.

Without pausing he led the way up the narrow tree fringed track. The bronc galloped without lessened speed until the footing became slithery with shale, and then Ben had to slacken pace. He sat upright, blew some of the dust from his mouth and lips, and drawled: "Stangle hides somewhere in these hills above Palermo. How come yuh never got the hombre? A good posse should have found that polecat's hideout before now."

The sheriff stood in his stirrups as his bay slithered on the shale. "Shore we bin after him. Most men figure he hides in some of the caves up here, but we bin in most of 'em an' nary a durned thing we did find! Ef he got himself a hideout in a cave, then the blamed thing takes some findin'."

Ben nodded. The steeply climbing path was degenerating into a faint deer track now, and would probably join up with the barely defined deer trail upon which he had first met Jeff Muldoon. All around were big rocky outcrops, cactus, junipers and scrub timber. It was desolate country up there, commending itself to no one except hunters and those hiding from the law. The terrain climbed all the while, with the deer trail leading and weaving round the jagged cliffs which had been hacked by some stroke of nature in the distant past.

Down below, on the edge of the hill encompassed by flat land lay Palermo. In the pale moonlight it looked deceptively innocent, the frame buildings huddling together as if for protection. It looked like a collection of toy boxes, with all its crudeness smoothed away under the pale light.

Finally Ben led the sheriff to the spot where he had met Jeff Muldoon.

"Met Stangle's hellion right here. He's a breed with an Irish name and look. Name o' Jeff Muldoon. Yuh know him, I reckon?"

"Shore. That grinning hombre is a killer. He jest likes killing like most men like likker and gambling and mebbe women. And Jeff like all them an' killing too. It's a quick drop to boothill for him when I get him."

"He packs two guns," commented Ben. He paused. "Yuh know, I figure Jed Stangle wasn't at the Flying T in that raid. He'd just left me in the Palermo Saloon where I'd got a room. I figure he didn't have time to make a raid on the other side of Toughgrass."

"Does it matter?" growled Sheriff Bainter. "His hellions shore enough pulled that pesky trick—now he's got Linda Harper. Makes me kinda mad to think o' it. She's just about the purtiest gal yuh ever saw in Toughgrass. Old Tom Wilson shore knew what he was doin' when he married her mother 'cause she was the smartest widder in Toughgrass."

"I hadn't time to tell yuh so far," began Ben, "but the way I figure it is Stangle wants the girl to force Tom Wilson's hand. Maybe he's tortured Tom and still he won't speak. But Tom Wilson won't stand for Linda being badly used."

"Yeah. I had a hunch that was it myself," admitted Hoot Bainter. "That polecat will stop

33

at nothin' to get the gold. Kin yuh imagine any man dragging a gal into this country jest tuh force an old man's hand? I'd give a year's pay to see Stangle and his hellions leave their bones in them Guadalupes."

"Reckon they'll chance that for the gold," commented Ben.

"Yeah. Guess any hombre would. D'yuh think we got a chance o' meeting up with them hombres tonight? An' if so how do yuh reckon to deal with 'em without getting recognised?"

"Look, Hoot, we got to take chances. We jest can't sit in town waiting for sunup while those rannigans have got that gal. I reckon Stangle must be mighty impatient by now and it's mighty important to get accepted by his gang and get inside his plans. If there's any shootin', I'll be around, but I'm not showin' myself. Anyway maybe we'll miss those rattlers in this half-light—we're jest have to take a chance, Hoot."

"Wal, cuss it, let's get on. Let's get them hoglegs of yourn shootin'!"

"That's my sentiments," said Ben grimly.

The gay sailing moon was an invaluable aid. Without its light they would have been unable to get very far. Even so, they were working on pure chance except for the fact that they were definitely in Jed Stangle's territory.

They were riding at walking pace round some giant buttes when they first saw the glint of fire through the scrub timber that clustered round the trail ahead. Ben immediately jigged his horse close to a flat face of rock and halted in the faint shadow it afforded. Sheriff Bainter lined up behind him.

"D'yuh think that's a camp fire?" hissed Ben.

"Maybe. I'm surprised if it is."

"How come? Those hombres have got to keep warm, same as any other galoot. And it gets kinda chilly in these hills after a warm day."

"Shore, but we bin up here before an' we couldn't see no fires."

Ben stared ahead at the small red glow. It flickered uncertainly, as if shadows crossed it intermittently. He could not make out anything else. There was intervening scrub timber, but he estimated the fire was beyond the timber and reckoned the flickering was caused by men passing before the fire.

"This is where we go kinda careful," he muttered. "There may be guards—if this is a camp. An' we may be on the wrong men. Could be some old hunter buildin' a fire to guard himself against those slinkin' wild cats."

But somehow he did not think it was a stray hunter. For one thing, most hunters or prospectors knew this to be Jed Stangle's territory, and they didn't care to horn in on trouble.

There was only one thing to do—get a bit closer. He jerked his head in a signal to Bainter, pulled his necktie up over his mouth and face, and tugged his hat down over his eyes. With his red shirt and grey sombrero, he figured he would look different from his usual appearance. And the light was uncertain—that was in his favour.

Ben led the way, taking his horse off the trail and wending a treacherous path through boulder strewn gullies towards the timber below. The rocks afforded partial cover, and it was better than riding along the narrow deer trail, which any guard would naturally cover.

And then, just as Ben was about to nudge his bronc out from behind a precariously balanced boulder as big as a shack, he saw the dim figure of a man sitting perched on a high rock at a point where the timber thinned and gave way to rock and shale.

If the guard had been really alert, Ben figured

he should be standing to get a better view of the trail. This hombre was taking it easy, and not even looking around.

He was sitting with his back against a smaller rock, rifle across his knees, making a cigarette. He was a typical border ruffian in nondescript shirt and Mexican sombrero.

Ben turned to Bainter. The sheriff sat his horse like a motionless tree on a still night.

"I'm goin' to get that hombre's clothes," said Ben in a whisper. "I reckon he's dead easy meat —if he stays like that taking it easy."

"Why his clothes?" grunted Hoot Bainter.

"Because they'll be mighty useful if we get to close quarters."

Ben dismounted and gave the reins to the sheriff. He went forward silently, making his way through the littered boulders. He slithered through foot-wide cracks with such expert feeling for cover that Sheriff Bainter, who was watching closely, was amazed. Hoot Bainter could not see Ben Harvey except for very brief intervals, and that was when Ben crept from one boulder to another, unavoidably crossing bare ground.

Ben negotiated the jagged terrain without so much as disturbing a rattler or a cactus. And he felt sure there were many rattlers in those rocky crevices—apart from the two-legged variety further ahead!

Ben was coming round from behind the guard. He was close enough now to hear the man as he sang some Mexican song under his breath. The fellow had probably been drinking.

Ben loosened his Colt into his right hand. He did not intend to fire it, but he figured it was heavy enough to lay that border breed flat on his rocky perch!

The last few yards were the worst. He had to be absolutely sure that not a pebble was dislodged as he crept cautiously nearer. And he was wondering too if the guard would rise to his feet for a brief survey of the surrounding land. If he did, Ben would have to be near a handy crevice.

Then Ben reached the shade of the big rock. He listened to the guard's song of boastful deeds, and grinned. Ben reached up, got a handhold. He put his foot in a crack, and moved softly up the face of the big rock. Ten feet above him the guard still sat, smoking his cigarette.

Ben held even his breath, and figured it was a ticklish moment. Idle the breed might be, but his ears were probably good enough to catch the slightest sound. It was a difficult job to climb ten feet of jagged rock without the faintest noise.

But Ben came to the top of the lookout and peered along. He was hardly four feet behind the guard's back.

Then the man, in some instinctive manner, sensed danger. The first warning to Ben was when the man stopped his low singing. He stopped abruptly. He was actually turning, scrambling to his feet when Ben heaved himself to the top and on to his feet. Ben made his rush all in one movement, flinging himself forward as he scrambled safely to the flat top of the rocky shelf. He caught the guard as the man was half turned and in a bad position for defence.

Ben's gun whipped up. The walnut stock came down, crushing through the guard's hat onto the man's skull. The border ruffian spreadeagled forward on his face.

Ben lugged him to the side of the rock and lowered him over and let him drop the ten feet. Ben leaped after him, and pulled him into the shadows. He did not want to be seen by other members of the gang, and the top of the rock was a bad place to start divesting the man of his clothes.

He was a dirty specimen, wearing a vest and shirt that only a breed would wear. Ben thought he could keep his jeans. They were just dark brown material like his own, but a lot dirtier.

The Texas Ranger took the Mexican sombrero and the man's vest and shirt. It was the work of a few minutes to undress the unconscious man, and by the time Ben had the man's wrists tied, he was stirring. Evidently he had a thicker skull than many, or the sombrero had blunted the blow.

Ben slipped his necktie over his face. It occurred to him that if the man was coming round, it would be a good idea to question him.

He shook the man, slapping his cheeks to bring back his senses. The guard groaned. Coming to a quick decision, Ben slung him over his shoulder and started back towards Sheriff Bainter.

He made the short trip a lot quicker than the first journey out. He scrambled up to the sheriff and dumped the guard at the law-man's feet.

"Here's our feller. Coming round, I guess. I want tuh ask him a few questions."

"Shore. Good idee—if it don't take too much time!" grunted Hoot Bainter.

"It'll be worth waiting a minute for news that might make a heck o' a difference. I got his mangy clothes off, anyway."

Ben dressed in the breed vest and shirt, pulling them over his own clothes. He did not want to leave any clothes lying around as clues. He took off his grey sombrero and stuffed it inside his two layers of shirts. He pulled the Mexican sombrero down over his eyes and looked up at Hoot Bainter, grinning.

"How do I look, Sheriff?"

"Like a durned mangy owl-hoot." The sheriff stared at the breed. "He's coming round. Yuh didn't hit him very hard, pardner."

"Must be tenderhearted, I guess." Ben kneeled down beside the man, and slapped the man's cheeks again. The breed opened his eyes and as he stared at Ben's masked face, fear shot through his eyes immediately.

"Talk, feller," hissed Ben. "Is that Jed Stangle's camp behind that fire? Were yuh the guard?"

"Damn and blast yuh!" The man went into a string of muttered curses.

Ben whipped a knife from his belt and held

41

it before the breed's eyes. The man gave a convulsive start. Ben pricked him without wasting further time. A tiny spurt of blood showed in the man's throat.

"We're wastin' no time with yuh, feller," hissed the Ranger. "Talk and talk fast. Now, is Jed Stangle camped here?"

"Don't use that knife! Shore it's Stangle's camp."

"Is it his regular hideout?"

The man hesitated, and Ben tickled him with the knife again. It was plain the fellow was not sure how far Ben was bluffing in his threat to kill him. But the outlaw probably judged the others by himself.

"Nope. This is jest a camp that Stangle reckons to pack up at sunup."

"All right. Never mind about his regular hideout. Has Stangle got the gal here?"

"Shore." The words came reluctantly, sullenly.

"And what about Tom Wilson?"

The owlhoot's eyes darted to Sheriff Bainter, noting the lawman's star.

"So yuh're Toughgrass men!" sneered the man. He stared hard at Ben, trying to penetrate

42

the masking necktie. "Why the disguise, amigo?"

"I asked yuh a question. Is Tom Wilson in this camp?" And Ben Harvey rubbed the point of his knife in the blood on the man's throat. He had the satisfaction of hearing an alarmed gasp from the man, though he knew he was not hurt.

"He ain't. The old fool is back at the hideout."

"All right, feller. Where's the hideout—just for future reference?"

Again the remorseless pressure of the pointed knife at his throat. The breed, looking into the glint of Ben's eyes, decided his captor was callous enough to kill him without a second's thought.

"Enough amigo! Yuh kin find Stangle's hideout in an arroyo at the foot o' Jacknife Hill."

Ben looked interrogatively at the sheriff.

"About an hour's ride," grunted Hoot Bainter.

"Good enough. We've got all we want tuh know," muttered Ben, and he quickly gagged the man. He tied his wrists to his ankles and dropped him into a large cleft in the rocks. The man was hidden until he was needed to be taken to Toughgrass for a trial.

They were by now as far as they could go with the horses. Ben tethered them with a rock tied to the dropped reins. He knew a well-trained cayuse would not move much with a heavy dropped rein keeping its head down.

The two men crept nearer to the camp, moving through the dry timber with the patience of Indians. It was slow work, but eventually they were close enough to see the camp fire and the men beside it.

There was no shack or cave. Apparently the outlaws were just camping, sitting round the fire with the horses in the trees. They had their ponchos unrolled and were lying on them with a blanket for cover and a saddle for a pillow. This was the life of the owl-hoot brigade.

Ben could clearly see the girl. She was sitting beside the fire, staring defiantly around her. She was wearing a leather riding skirt and boots, a buckskin shirt and a hat of blue felt, and even from a distance she looked mighty pretty in the fire-light. But what held Ben's attention—and Sheriff Bainter's—was the hulking fellow who stood before her, teasing her. She stared angrily at him, and then darted quick glances at the other amused outlaws. If she was appealing for help, she was doomed to disappointment.

The big man leaned forward and held her chin. He laughed coarsely, and Ben could hear the guffaw. The man made as if to kiss the girl, but he got a surprise instead.

Her hands were tied evidently, for they were behind her back, but her feet were free. As the hulking ruffian came close to her, guffawing all the time, she lashed out with her boots. They were not big boots, but they brought a yell of pain as they caught the outlaw on a tender part of his shin.

Ben saw the girl's lips part in a smile of satisfaction, and he had the momentary thought that she was certainly a spirited girl.

But he tightened his lips grimly a second later. It was all he could do not to start up and run into the camp there and then. As the big man got over his pain, he came forward threateningly and struck the girl hard on the head with his fist.

He had plenty of weight. The girl slowly fell over and lay still. The man glared at her and slouched away. There was no response from his comrades except callous amusement.

"I'm going into the camp," said Ben abruptly. "They'll think—"

He paused as a man ambled out of the fire's glare and plodded down to the trail towards them. Ben and the sheriff waited. The man carried a rifle carelessly, and he was making for the rocky lookout post.

Ben nudged Hoot Bainter.

"That's the guard's relief. We've got tuh silence that hombre and quick. We'll get him as he comes through that gully."

They waited about five minutes. Yard by yard the man ambled towards them, on his way to relieve his pal. Then, with one movement, the two men fell upon him. The rifle was knocked from his grasp, and he was crushed to the ground without so much as a gasp.

Ben took him into the shadows of the timber and bound him with his necktie. The outlaw was gagged and thrust into a crevice overhung with cactus.

"This is a good chance," whispered Ben as he crouched with the sheriff under cover. "I'm goin' tuh walk into the camp—jest as if I was coming off guard duty. It's a good gamble the owlhoots will think I'm jest the guard coming in."

Taking the rifle, holding it loosely in his arms he began to amble forward. He did not hurry or make any nervous movements—for he was not feeling a bit nervous. He just felt a cool, grim anticipation. Although he did not want to give away his identity, in a sense he would relish a chance to blaze hot lead at some of these galoots.

He came through the trees and entered the area of the camp. No one looked at him. They seemed a pretty indolent crew, but appearances were often deceptive. Maybe they thought they were safe.

Ben strolled on, head well down, his hat covering his forehead and eyes with shadows. He looked a typical border ruffian in his dirty range clothes. Ben shuffled past the fire, turning his head slowly away from the blaze. He moved up to the girl. He saw clearly that she was still unconscious from the blow the ruffian had struck.

Ben dropped his rifle deliberately. He bent down as if to pick it up, hardly a foot distant from the girl.

But when he straightened like a bent sapling suddenly released, he was holding the girl in his arms. He sprang for the other side of the camp.

His powerful legs took him in long leaps to the shadows in the surrounding scrub timber. Within five or six seconds he was out of the camp fire's red glare, and the men had hardly reacted.

But he knew they would. So far it was all so simple.

A Colt barked at him, and the bullet thudded into the hole of a nearby tree. It was the first bit of flying lead. He plunged to the right to upset any marksman who might be aiming at him. The girl was a light burden in his strong arms at the moment.

Then, on the other side of the camp, a gun roared. Ben guessed it was Sheriff Bainter, who had agreed to cover him. The gun boomed again and again, and in answer a perfect fusilade of shots rang out. The owlhoots were roused and shooting now!

Ben knew he had to make a wide detour inside the scrub and at the same time he had to avoid barging into the outlaws' camp. He felt several bullets sing past him and knew he was being chased. The trouble was he could not stop and exchange lead, for the girl in his arms made that sort of trouble-shooting difficult.

He had to get to the horses, near the sheriff. And he had to get the girl away.

He swung off through an ancient, dried watercourse with an instinctive sense that it would bring him round to Bainter and the horses. Two bullets whanged uncomfortably close.

The pebbly watercourse afforded some cover, and he made good speed. He could hear shots being exchanged to his right, and he hoped Sheriff Bainter was making out all right.

Then he suddenly came clear of the scrub and was among the rocks and shale again. He could see the horses but only indistinctly. He glimpsed a flash of flame from a spot among the rocks. Hoot Bainter was still doing all right.

Ben came down on the sheriff's right side, taking full advantage of the sandstone rocks standing there like sentinels. He felt he was clear now—at least no lead was coming his way —and he was too far to the side to get in the way of the lead the sheriff was exchanging with the outlaws.

Presently he reached the clump of timber where the horses were tethered. The animals were inclined to be a bit spooked with the gunplay, but he grabbed their reins. He lowered the girl to the ground, paused and gave a low shout to Hoot Bainter.

The sheriff heard him immediately, for he began to retreat keeping his head well down in the gully. In seconds he had scrambled to Harvey.

"So yuh got the girl! Doggone me—yuh got the nerve of ten men. Good fer yuh. Let's get movin'."

Ben cut the rope from the girl's wrists, and she stirred.

"Get on yore hoss," he snapped to Bainter. "An' take the girl down the trail to Toughgrass."

"What about yuh?"

"I'll ride behind and exchange a slug or two with these gents. I'll cover up for yuh, and bring that trussed-up hombre we have in the crevice over yonder."

"All right! Yuh shore like yuh own way. Blame me, ef I had yuh as my depity, yuh'd be giving me orders!" growled Bainter.

Nevertheless he climbed to his horse and took the girl up with him. She was stirring.

"I've got two points tuh bear in mind," Ben rapped. "I don't want tuh be recognised by anybody—and I include the gal. And I figure

50

it's a good idee to get that breed down to your lock-up for questioning. He might not've been speakin' the truth about Jacknife Hill."

A bullet pinging into a rock and raising dust galvanised the sheriff.

"I get yuh. Ef yuh bring that breed down, drop him in the cottonwoods outside o' Toughgrass."

"Sure. Now git, Sheriff. I got to get myself back tuh my room in the Palermo Saloon. I've got to make out I've been there all night."

Without another word Bainter spurred his horse and disappeared down the shale-strewn deer trail. Ben watched a brief second. He had a sense of inward satisfaction when he realised that Jed Stangle's plans had been foiled so far.

He wheeled abruptly and ran at a crouch to the crevice where the breed had been dropped. He went on his knees and peered down. The man was still there and evidently tired of struggling. He did not move as Ben pulled him out by his bound feet.

And then the Texas Ranger saw why the man had not moved and why he would not move again.

A rattler had got the man as he lay in the crevice. He had been bitten on the face. It was blue and distended, and there was an expression of sheer terror on the man's ugly features.

Ben dropped him with a feeling of revulsion he could not control. It was a rotten way to die even for a murderous renegade.

As Ben moved swiftly away he thought suddenly that at least the man would be unable to talk to Jed Stangle.

Ben jumped to the bronc and rode away at a hard pace. A gun roared lead at him as if in parting. Ben twisted and fired back at random. He knew spitting lead often had a deterring effect even when it went wide.

He let the bronc have its head as they went down the twisting trail. He wondered if he might catch up with the slower sheriff, but he did not think so. And at the bottom of the trail, where it broadened through usage, he turned and waded his bronc through the creek and went on towards Palermo.

The town still looked quiet under the pale moonlight, though he knew that the saloons were packed to suffocation.

He dismounted at a safe distance from the town. He slapped the bronc's flanks and the horse went galloping down the trail to Toughgrass. It would go right back to the livery at Hoot Bainter's place.

Whipping off the Mexican sombrero, and the vest and shirt, he stuffed them in a clump of mesquite. He pulled his grey sombrero down over his eyes and, grinning a little, made his way into the town. He avoided the main street and walked carefully between shacks and stores. The moon was still sailing aloft, but it had travelled a long way since he had set out.

He found the back of the saloon deserted.

He got through the half-open window and slid into the room. The oil-lamp was still burning low as he had left it, and the chair was still jammed against the door.

4

Hilltop Hideout

NEXT morning Ben rose early, shook the sleep from his eyes and went downstairs. There had been no alarms during the night. He was glad he had got the sleep in because he never knew what the next twenty-four hours might bring.

After he had sluiced water over his arms, face and chest from a tub in the yard, he ran his hand over his bristly beard and grinned. Normally he was a man who liked to shave in a country where shaving was not the rule, but he knew he would appear more like the usual paid gunman if he wandered round with a growth on his chin.

He got a meal at the Chinese restaurant, and then stood on the boardwalk eyeing the activity of the lawless junk heap of a town. Buckboards clattered by and an oxen-drawn freight team lumbered up the main stem driven by a Mexican. But most of the carousing cowboys of the previous night had ridden back to the distant spreads.

Ben strolled along to the livery, saw that his bay was ready and fed, then went back to the saloon and contacted the bartender.

"I want to pay my bill, feller," he said. "I might be back and I might not. For yore information I'm joining a pardner, but yuh needn't tell that to any meddlin' sheriffs!"

The bartender grinned.

"Yeah. Reckon yuh could do worse." He took the bills Ben handed him. "Appears this pardner o' yourn got hisself on to a good proposition—not mentionin' no names!"

Ben gave him a cold grin and walked out. Muscles rippled under the soft gaberdine of his green shirt. His black stetson was good and helped him effect a swagger. His twin Colts lay low in shiny holsters, their walnut stocks not fancy, but polished with usage. Few men in the outlaw town would fail to notice his guns.

The sun was climbing like a brassy galleon in the sky. In the town there was dust and sweat. Up in the hills it would be cooler, Ben knew. Apart from the scrub and the rocks and dusty cactus, there would be patches or orange where the chollas and opuntias swayed in the slight breeze. There would be rattlers in the rocks, and deer fleeing infrequently among the trees and patches of grass.

Ben was taking all his possessions with him, but not very far. He had his red shirt and grey sombrero stuffed in a bag which he had left at the livery. The bag was knotted tight: he trusted no one in Palermo. Once out of town he intended to bury the hat and shirt in some sandy patch and cover it with rocks. Maybe he had not been noticed wearing the red shirt and grey sombrero in his rides last night, but he was not taking the slightest chance. As a special agent of the Rangers, he took chances—but only those involving gun-play. A man might expect to die in a gun battle, but not because his shirt was recognised.

Harvey rode his bay out of Palermo as the sun, becoming even fiercer, created stinks in the garbage among the back yards. This was Western Texas, and only a hundred miles away the desert began, leading right into the terrible Guadalupes.

He rode slowly, letting the cayuse have its easy gait. So far he had been accepted by Jed Stangle, but there might be fast riding later on.

The broad trail thinned, leaving the mesquite

and sage behind and assuming a rocky character. There was plenty of shale for long lengths of the climbing track as it wound its way through the scrub and junipers and the patches of cholla cactus now bursting into brilliant flower. If the hill country was no use to ranchers or nesters, it was at least a change from the never-ending flatness of the plains below.

Ben let the horse pick its way. He was in no hurry. He had decided he would bump into the trail guard somewhere sooner or later. After which, apparently, he would be taken to Stangle's main hideout in Jacknife Hill—unless the breed who had died of rattler poisoning was lying.

Ben left the reins on the saddle horn, and with a small piece of rag he cleaned his Colts.

It was just another precaution he was taking. He did not want some awkward customer suspecting his guns had been fired recently.

He was concerned about Tom Wilson, though he had never met him. He was wondering if Stangle would renew his pressure on the old-timer now that Linda Harper was back at her home. It seemed likely, and Ben did not like the set-up. It looked as if his first duty should be to get Wilson away to safety, if he could, and then turn to effecting the capture of Stangle and his outlaws.

Ben rode past the three massive junipers beside which he had met Jeff Muldoon the other day, but there was no sign of a guard. He carried on, noting he was in a different area from the spot where Stangle's men had camped last night. Entering a grove of sycamores, which sent their branches to the sky, their leaves spreading coolly over the trail, Ben thought it was a pleasant place for a man to halt and lie down. Under these giant trees the air was drowsy, and birds had made a colony in the swaying tops. It would sure be nice to halt, letting the bay crop grass and to stretch himself out.

Ben resisted the temptation of the lazy air in the sycamore glade and rode on. He came into the open again, rounded a sudden coulee and saw a horse jig into hiding behind some rock. Ben rode on without hesitating, his hands lightly before him holding the reins in first-class riding style, but ready to flash like lightning to the shiny Colts.

The rider was hiding, watching him in some way, probably through a crevice in the rock that Ben could not see from a distance.

As he rounded the coulee, he saw Jeff Muldoon, astride a gelding, grinning warily as Ben halted his horse, facing him.

"Yuh waiting for me, hombre?" asked Ben mildly.

The other nodded.

"Shore. Stangle wants tuh see yuh."

"Yuh taking me to headquarters?"

"Yeah." Jeff Muldoon thrust fingers into a vest pocket and brought out the "makings." As he rolled the cigarette deftly, his Irish parentage showed in those glinting, grinning eyes, but he was Mexican owlhoot in everything else. There were *caballeros* South of the Border with pride in their estates and their honour, but Jeff Muldoon was not one of these.

"Wal, let's git goin'." And Ben nudged his horse, turning its head.

"Hear any news in town last night?" asked Jeff Muldoon casually.

"News? No—I was asleep most o' the time after yuh left my room. What news?"

Jeff Muldoon rode abreast, blew smoke over his horse's bobbing mane.

"Stangle's play got busted up last night," he said briefly. "Thought yuh might o' heerd about it. News always get around Palermo."

"How come it was busted?"

"Wal, Jed sent a crew over tuh the Flying T tuh pick up that gal, Linda Harper. She's Tom Wilson's step-daughter, an' Stangle wanted her so he could make that old cuss speak."

"Did they git the gal?"

"Shore—got her all right. But thet blamed sheriff from Toughgrass and another hombre rode into the camp later and took the gal off."

"Say, what sorta outfit does Stangle run?" demanded Ben harshly. "Yuh reckon two galoots walk into a camp and get the gal back —just like that! I figured Stangle was running a tough crew."

Jeff Muldoon spat dust.

"I wasn't at the camp. Cain't say how it come about, but I can tell yuh Stangle's sorer than a mountain bear. He figured tuh make a start today towards gittin' that gold. Everythin' was ready fer a trip into them Guadalupes—hosses an' grub—if he'd made Tom Wilson talk."

"Does he aim to take the old gallot along?"

"Shore. The old catamount is needed tuh locate the bonanza. Could be he aims tuh trick Stangle."

"I seen men hazed before when it comes tuh tracking another galoot's gold," growled Ben.

"May be. But Stangle's the hombre tuh deal with this feller's gold."

Ben gave an audible grunt as if to signify that he felt dubious about many things.

They rode on in silence for a while, leaving the deer trail completely. They went through rocky defiles and across sandy draws, the hills were swallowing them in their never-ending folds.

"When do we hit camp?" growled Ben eventually, drawing abreast of the other as they sat their horses on the ridge of a steeply sloping hill. "Sure would like tuh see a bit o' flat ground. Where is this camp?"

"Plenty o' ridin' yet. Ever heard o' Jacknife Hill?"

Ben was about to nod when he checked himself. As far as Jeff Muldoon was concerned he had never heard of the place!

"Can't say I have. I don't know this territory."

"Yuh'll not need tuh know it ef Stangle makes that old cuss talk today—an' I figure he is. Yuh're pretty lucky coming in with Jed Stangle right now. Orta be something good for the bunch when we locate that gold."

"Ever bin in the Guadalupes?" asked Ben.

"Naw. Yuh wouldn't catch me in that hell-hole. But I reckon I'll make the trip wi' Stangle if he gets the location from Wilson."

"Has Stangle been persuadin' the oldster?" asked Ben significantly.

Muldoon laughed callously.

"Shore did. Nearly kilt him. Blamed ef I ever saw any hombre take so much punishment. Seems like he jest wouldn't speak. All he ever did was groan an' then pass out. Stangle sloshed him wi' water a few times and put a knife on the old idjut's face again. Or some wood splinters under his fingernails—yuh know the old Injun tricks! But that old galoot jest took it all. Stangle couldn't go too far, he wanted the old coot to be able tuh take him tuh the Guadalupes."

Ben Harvey felt like ramming Muldoon's drawling words down his stringy throat. Mentally he marked Jeff Muldoon off for just retribution some day—along with Stangle and his outfit.

The border ruffian chuckled again.

"Yeah. I remember when some feller said tuh Stangle tuh cut Tom Wilson's tongue out. That was this hombre's idee of making the old-timer talk! Stangle nearly kilt the feller who suggested it!"

"Must ha' plenty o' iron, this old feller," commented Ben.

Jeff Muldoon nodded, drawled, "Yeah. But what the hell good will it do him?"

Ben had no comment, and they rode on across monotonous hills and gullies of shale and sand.

Then after some twenty minutes Jeff Muldoon said, "Yuh can see Jacknife Hill better now. Over there. Aain't very high, but it's a natural hideout. Got water and grass for the hosses. Stangle fixed up a cave better'n a bunkhouse!"

Inwardly Ben noted that the dead breed had been speaking the truth.

"There's a fast ridin' trail into Toughgrass," went on Jeff Muldoon, "but Stangle said I had tuh bring yuh thisaway."

Ben said harshly, "Why? Don't he trust me? Why come the slow way?"

"Can't say, hombre. Jed Stangle doesn't tell me all his thoughts. Maybe he aims tuh show yuh things gradual-like."

Ben nodded. That could be. Stangle had to be cautious. It was probably born in him.

Soon the terrain changed. They went along rocky pathways, skirting ravines, struggling up bare rocky slopes until at last they were on a big ledge of Jacknife Hill pitted here and there with naturally tunnelled mouths of caves which were probably the haunts of eagles. The ledge was hidden by dense clumps of pines, sycamores and cedars, and the whole place was a lofty eyrie for Stangle's followers of the owlhoot trail. Ben noticed the stream which bubbled in a thin trickle. Evidently it came from some high altitude and went down into the basin to form Palermo Creek.

"This is it," said Muldoon, turning his cayuse to a well-defined horse track which led right into the clearing immediately before a cave mouth.

There were men about and they turned to stare at Ben and Muldoon. Smoke was rising from a fire under an adobe oven, and a Mexican was cooking.

Ben knew he was right in the thick of the outlaws' stronghold now. He had to watch his step. One false move and he would be shot or knifed without compunction.

He studied the place as he rode in, though outwardly he appeared to be casual. He reckoned he could locate the hideout again, now that he had seen it, but realised it would need a lot of men to shoot the outlaws out of the place.

Still that was the future. He knew his intentions; plans could be formulated at a minute's notice. There was no other way.

There were shouts of greeting.

"Hyar, Jeff!"

"Hyar, stranger!"

Then Stangle strode out of the cave.

"Howdy, Harvey," he said. "Come right on over here."

He gestured to the cave and strode back without looking further at Ben. The Ranger dismounted, hitched the reins over a tie rail, and walked after Stangle. He was well aware of the shrewd glances that came his way. Jeff Muldoon walked off in another direction, and Ben caught up with Stangle in the cave's mouth.

He was in a wide cave with smooth sides and a floor of sand. Ben saw immediate evidence of Jed Stangle's villainy in the stack of bullion boxes stored at the mouth. Some time in the past, the gang had evidently attacked a stagecoach loaded with bullion, for the boxes bore the words, "Toughgrass County Bank."

Seemingly the money had already been dissipated, and Stangle was after the gold mine in the Guadalupes.

In a naturally convenient angle of the cave wall, a rough shanty had been built, and towards this Stangle walked heavily. He turned, beckoning to Ben, and as Ben hurried up, Stangle pushed open a door and led the way into the shack.

The grey light, filtering along the cave from the mouth thirty feet away, made the inside of the shack shadowy, but Ben was quick to see a crouched figure of a man squatting in a corner. Also, facing the man, was Rocky Creel.

Rocky Creel turned a grim face to Ben as he entered, and did not bother to nod or recognise the other.

Ben looked interestedly at the man in the corner of the shack. The oldster was in a pitiable condition. He was covered in dirt, and his whiskers sprouted fiercely round a weatherbeaten face which showed some purple bruises. He lay as if conserving his strength, but his bright eyes glared up at the others.

"Yuh won't get nuthin' outa me!" he cackled.

"Ef we get nothin' out yuh, we'll kill yuh!" hissed Rocky Creel.

Old Tom Wilson peered at Ben.

"Brought another hellion tuh see me!" he spat. "Ain't seen this yellerbelly before!"

Ben grinned at Stangle, stirred Wilson with his foot. But he hardly touched the old-timer even though his riding-boot callously lifted the old man. But all the same he had to make some show of being with Stangle.

"This is the old galoot, Harvey," said Stangle. "This hombre knows where there is plenty of gold—enough for all the gang tuh take away on a horse each. But the old fool won't talk."

"Care tuh let me work on him?" queried Ben.

Stangle stroked his red moustache, looked sneeringly at Ben.

"What th'hell d'yuh think yuh can do when I can't make him talk? I tell yuh this feller aims tuh be killed before he'll talk."

Ben shrugged.

"Have it yore own way. I only take orders if I'm working with you."

Secretly he was glad Stangle had not taken him up on the offer. But he had made the offer to impress the outlaw leader. As a newcomer, the others might be somewhat wary and suspicious of him.

"He's shore got it figgered out," went on Stangle sneeringly. "He's ready tuh take plenty o' punishment, and he knows I can't go too far. Ef we're goin' into them Guadalupes, we don't want no cripples."

"Especially the hombre who's goin' tuh show yuh the mine," commented Ben.

He was glad of the opportunity to put in a few words that might influence Stangle to lay off Tom Wilson.

"Shore. But I got other ways o' makin' men talk," said Stangle. "I nearly got his stepdaughter, but some blamed fools let that pesky sheriff from Toughgrass horn in."

"Jeff Muldoon was tellin' me all about it on the trail up," said Ben.

Jed Stangle's eyes gleamed.

"But he didn't tell yuh that I'm goin' tuh get that gal again, did he?"

Ben looked surprised.

"Yuh're figuring tuh get the gal up here after last night?"

"Shore. It's still the best way tuh make this old hombre talk."

Rocky Creel glanced narrowly at Ben Harvey.

"Yuh kinda billed tuh get the gal," he sneered.

"Me? Yuh meant yuh want me tuh git the gal?" Ben swung to Stangle with the question on his lips.

The bandit leader walked a few paces thoughtfully, fingering his bristly moustache. He flicked a calculating look at Ben.

"Yeh. Yuh shore look like the right hombre for a job that needs guts. I'd send Rocky Creel, but I'm givin' you the chance. Git that gal for me, Harvey, an' yuh're on tuh something good. Remember, this feller got plenty o' gold outa them Guadalupes, and according tuh the things he useta say when he bought the Flying T spread, there's enough gold for the lot of us. But I figger only the gal will make him talk. That so, old-timer?"

Stangle kicked at Wilson and the old man curled up in agony as the heavy boot connected. He seemed to buckle and hold his breath, as if fighting the pain down. Ben mentally chalked up another notch against Stangle.

There was no answer from the oldster, and

Stangle went on, "I was talking with Creel about yuh. We figger there'll be a guard on that gal now. They're sorta on the lookout, now that they've been warned, so yuh'll have tuh get past those Flying T rannies. I don't know how yuh'll git the gal, but I want yuh to try. Yuh can take Jeff Muldoon with yuh."

"Yuh mean yuh want jest the two of us tuh snatch that gal from the Flying T?" said Ben slowly.

"That's the idee. Jest the two of yuh. And now."

"In daylight?"

"Shore. I said now—soon as yuh kin git goin'. Git that blamed gal up here and we'll make the old feller talk. I want tuh get started on this trip intuh the Guadalupes—the sooner the better."

"Yuh're the boss," said Ben quickly. "But I wish tuh hell yuh'd told me this before I rode up thet long trail with Muldoon. We could've got started without ridin' up here."

Stangle's lips almost lapsed into a grin.

"Yuh got an ornery nature. That's why I got yuh to ride the long trail up here. There's a fast trail tuh Toughgrass, an' yuh kin take that trail when yuh go down this time. Yuh kin see I'm boss o' this outfit, Harvey, and ef I told yuh to ride round the rim o' hell, yuh'd do it."

Ben slowly felt in his shirt pocket for the "makings."

"Yuh're the boss," he said again.

Stangle strode to the door.

"Shore. Git Muldoon and git started. Ef yuh don't come back we'll figger yuh full of lead or taking the quick drop tuh boothill."

Ben lighted his cigarette.

"An' what do we get fer this?"

"Gold," said Stangle harshly. "It's lead or gold, feller. Take yore choice."

Rocky Creel moved closer to Ben. His face was inscrutable, but his eyes were hate-filled. Ben stared back. He realised Stangle's *segundo* nursed an instinctive dislike of him. It was the animosity of men who just naturally hated each other on sight.

"Maybe yuh don't like working for Stangle after all," said Creel. "Maybe yuh don't care much for yore first job!"

"It's a good job," said Ben coolly. "What makes yuh think I don't like it?"

Creel stared savagely, momentarily baffled for words. Stangle said, "Move to it, Harvey. Creel hates yore guts."

"That's too bad!" drawled Ben.

Stangle jerked his head impatiently.

"Just forget it. Git started with Muldoon. Take Winchesters and anythin' yuh want. We got plenty o' stuff. Change yore hat and shirt, feller. That stylish stetson might git yuh recognised before yuh hit the Flying T. Jeff Muldoon knows all the trails around here, so yuh'll be all right. I figger yuh're the hombre tuh shoot yuh way into the Flying T if needed. Don't bank on Jeff takin' too many risks."

And Jed Stangle strode away down the cave, his heavy boots kicking up sand with every step. Creel glanced covertly at Ben.

"Did yuh suggest this little gunsmoke party tuh Stangle?" drawled Ben.

The *segundo* parted his thin lips in a sneer.

"See yuh when yuh come back, hombre— maybe!"

And he strode after Stangle with the attitude of a man who is secretly pleased with events.

Ben walked slowly forward a few yards. He kept his eyes on Rocky Creel's back.

Plans were flashing through his mind. His real job was to get Tom Wilson out of Stangle's hands. That was the first consideration, but it seemed impossible to carry out at the moment.

72

He was close enough to the man he had come to rescue, but right now there was no way of getting him out of Stangle's stronghold. For a moment Ben thought of cutting the old-timer free, and then shooting his way out. But he knew it was simply impossible. The outlaws would get him and the old-timer sure as drought in summer.

Ben suddenly quickened his step. There was but one plan which would be any good in this situation. He would have to get a large posse into these hills now that he knew Stangle's hideout.

His best bet was to ride down with Jeff Muldoon and then—somehow—get to Sheriff Bainter all information about the camp in Jacknife Hill.

Anyway, Stangle was not giving him much time to waste in the outlaw stronghold. He had just ridden in and now he was destined to go out on this expedition to kidnap Linda Harper.

Ben went along and found Jeff Muldoon. As he came up to the Irish-Mexican, the man turned disgruntled eyes to him.

"So we get the risky job!" said the breed.

"Stangle told yuh?"

"Shore. We have to get thet gal—in daylight,

amigo!" Jeff came close to Ben, his black eyes scowling. "I tell yuh it is impossible. Those Flying T waddies will be all over the place, and we'll get lead poisoning."

"Yuh don't like the job?"

"Nope. Yuh durned right, I don't! I figger Stangle is plumb mad tuh think about it. I notice he ain't agoin' down himself tuh start trouble-shooting with them Flying T rannies!"

Ben hid a grin.

"Yuh want me to tell Stangle this?" he queried.

Fear flicked across Muldoon's sallow face for a second like trailing leaves across a horse's back.

"Forget it, *amigo!* You know Stangle is a hombre who can't take a joke."

"Then there's nothin' more tuh say," said Ben. "I see yuh got yuh hoss ready, anyway. I got orders tuh change my hat and shirt. Stangle doesn't like it. Yuh know where I can git spares?"

"Shore. We got a whole heap o' duds when we raided some freight wagons a bit back. I'll show yuh, and yuh kin help yuhself."

Jeff Muldoon showed Ben stacks of goods heaped in a dry cave with a sandy floor. There was food enough for months, clothes of all sorts, boots, saddles and bedding. Ben selected an orange-red shirt with a grey vest to cover it. He changed quickly, and finished by putting on a low-crowned black hat and tying a new yellow neckchief under his chin.

"Kinda looks a natty outfit," he observed. "How'd yuh like it, Muldoon? Maybe I'll look a stranger tuh Toughgrass citizens—till they get a good look at me!"

But Muldoon only scowled. It was plain he did not relish the task Stangle had given him.

In the cave was a box of rifles all in perfect condition, and a case of ammunition. Ben made a note of this for the sake of possible future events. He selected a Winchester, wondering why he was bothering to be so methodical because he certainly had no intention of using the rifle against Flying T cowboys.

Still he had to convince Stangle. He wished he had another companion with him—a hombre who would take a chance and start blazing lead. But one man had no chance. The outlaws could surround him and pick him off at their convenience.

He rode out of the stronghold with Jeff Muldoon, to the accompaniment of waves from the other lounging outlaws. Stangle and Creel stood on a ledge and watched them ride down an open trail, the fast trail to Toughgrass.

Harvey felt he knew what was in Stangle's mind in sending two men to kidnap the girl. He probably figured that they might be killed, and in this event he was only losing one man and a newcomer who had yet to prove his loyalty and worth. If they successfully brought the girl back to Jacknife Hill, then the venture was a good one. There was no time limit, but Stangle had made it plain that he wanted the girl that day.

Muldoon led the way and they rode down the well-defined trail at a good gallop. Although the trail twisted pretty frequently, it was possible to rowel a cayuse most of the way.

After an hour they came down to the foothills that crept down on Palermo.

"Yuh care for a drink?" asked Jeff Muldoon.

"Why?" asked Ben.

"I feel it might be the last drink this side o' hell," snapped the breed.

"Yuh kin back out, if yuh like," said Ben calmly.

"What th'hell d'yuh mean?"

"Jest what I say, *amigo*. Yuh don't seem tuh

like the job. Wal, yuh kin go get yuh a drink in Palermo, an' I'll git the gal."

"By yuhself?" Muldoon was incredulous.

"Shore. It ain't so hard. In fact maybe I got more chance operatin' on my own."

"If yuh tryin' tuh insult me—" began the breed nastily.

"Don't be a fool. Yuh needn't say anythin' tuh Stangle. Git yuhself a drink if you like, and I'll ride on."

Muldoon halted his horse uncertainly. He looked down at Palermo, sweltering in the afternoon sun. There was activity in the lawless town, and the breed was visualising the whiskey and gambling obtainable in the saloons.

"Tell yuh what," urged Ben. "Yuh kin get yuhself a drink while I ride out to the Flying T and scout around. Maybe I might see something good in the setup out there, an' I'll ride back. Then we can make a plan—go out and kidnap the girl."

"Yeah. That's better." Jeff Muldoon visibly brightened. "Guess one feller can ride through to the Flying T better'n two. Then we figure out something, an' we git moving."

Ben wheeled his horse.

"All right, hombre. I'll be back pretty soon. Don't git too much o' that firewater!"

"I cain't git too much!" boasted Muldoon.

Ben smiled grimly as he rode away. At the last moment, he twisted in his saddle and saw the breed riding down the trail to the town.

The trail was clear now for a fast ride to Toughgrass and a word in Sheriff Hoot Bainter's ear.

Ben Harvey had it planned. While Jeff Muldoon was waiting for him to return, a posse would set out for the hills and three men would ride into Palermo and pick the breed up. It would be Toughgrass jail for Jeff Muldoon that night! The Irish-Mexican ruffian was having his last drink for a long time!

Ben could have turned a gun on the breed and simply brought him into Toughgrass, but there was a reason why he did not. It was possible something might go wrong. If Jeff was picked up by Sheriff Bainter, it could be attributed to chance and good luck on the sheriff's part. That would still let Ben out of suspicion if Jed Stangle's gang escaped the posse, and Ben thought he could rejoin Stangle later with some plausible tale showing how he had escaped the lawmen.

Jeff Muldon had simply played into his hands!

Ben Harvey rode fast to Toughgrass. He passed other riders but they took no notice. His big bay was a fast mount and went along with flying hoofs.

He was taking a short-cut, a straight line which took him within the boundary of the Flying T spread, when as he passed a large clump of cottonwoods he noticed a bunch of riders.

They noticed him, too, for men and horses turned. The bunch of waddies had been on a wire-fence extending job, but they stopped when they saw Ben's flying horse.

And then the Ranger caught a glimpse of a girl on a pinto. She was sitting like an expert horsewoman, and she had not been immediately noticeable. It was Linda Harper, and apparently she had been seeing the waddies on to the job.

Ben's big horse was taking him speedily over the mesa when suddenly there was a shout. A man bawled, "That's the hombre we chased outa Toughgrass!"

Ben cursed. He heard another man shout.

"After him! Yuh're durned right—he joined up wi' Stangle's outfit!"

"Git him!"

Ben swore under his breath again. He had not anticipated this although he had reckoned to encounter a bit of trouble in Toughgrass if stopped before he reached Bainter's office.

Would these hombres believe his story?

There was only one answer: he would have to rein his cayuse and explain.

A shot sang out and Ben reined in grimly. He wheeled the big bay and cantered back to the men. His hands were well before him and his sudden act evidently surprised the group.

"Wal, doggone me! Shore got the nerve!"

"Yeah. Maybe he's a tricky hombre. Watch him!"

Ben heard the comments and he tensed worriedly. It was damned bad luck to encounter trouble like this, especially when he wanted to get to Sheriff Bainter with all speed. But he would have to explain, and even that was not so good when it meant disclosing the story of his line-up with Stangle.

The Flying T waddies bunched around him, halting their horses within a few feet of Ben.

Linda Harper rode up and stared at him. There was grimness on her pretty face.

They were all around him and they were all staring mighty hard.

5

Cottonwood Conference

A BIG leathery-faced man took the lead in questioning Ben.

"Yuh're name o' Harvey. I was in the posse that chased yuh outa Toughgrass the other day. I recognise yuh."

Ben nodded.

"That's right," he began. "But there's a lot to explain. I—"

The leathery-faced man said disgustedly. "Yeah, there's always a lot to explain. I'm Bantley—ramrod at the Flying T."

"Sure—" began Ben again.

"We heerd yuh joined up with Stangle," accused another man.

Linda Harper edged her pinto closer and said deliberately, "If you're one of Stangle's men, I hate you."

There were low growls of approval at the girl's words. A man shouted, "You know what

82

we do wi' owlhoots! We put a hangnoose round their necks."

"Not without listening to their explanations, surely?" said Ben sharply.

"Explanations! Aw, that's good!" jeered a waddy.

"I'm ridin' tuh see Sheriff Bainter right now," shouted Ben grimly. "Why else d'yuh think I'm on the trail to Toughgrass?"

"Maybe yuh aim to pull another hold-up!"

Ben breathed grimly, facing the enraged men and the girl. He took more than one glance at Linda Harper, amazed at her prettiness even in this dangerous moment. He had his badge of the Texas Rangers in a secret pocket of his belt, and he could show it as a last resort.

"Bantley, I make yuh a fair offer," he appealed. "Ride with me into Toughgrass— take my guns if yuh wish—and we'll see Sheriff Bainter. I got a story tuh tell yuh, but I'd like tuh tell it in front of Sheriff Bainter. If I'm what yuh think, wal, yuh got me cold. What y'yuh think o' that?"

Jack Bantley was an honest man and a fine, reliable foreman, tough as cowhide. He hesitated, weighing Ben's words in his mind.

"Seems fair enough," he said.

But a chorus of growls came from the other waddies, and Linda Harper made no comment. She simply stared at Ben with cold anger in her lovely blue eyes. Ben could understand. From all accounts Tom Wilson had been like a second father to her, and so she would hate anyone remotely connected with Stangle's outfit.

Jack Bantley looked round.

"What d'yuh rannies think?" he asked. "I think he oughta be given the benefit of his words. But yuh got opinions, too."

"String him up now!" bawled a voice.

"Shore! We got plenty o' rope and there's plenty o' cottonwoods!"

"Yuh can't take the law into yuh own hands," growled Bantley. "I got tuh tell yuh that men."

Linda Harper sat on her stocky little pinto with burning eyes in a face that had gone suddenly pale.

"Yuh can string him up for me," she said in a tense tone as the hubbub subsided. "I hate him—hate all of them!"

And she turned her head away as if to hide sudden tears.

Ben took a deep, grim breath.

"I ask yuh once more tuh give me a chance.

I'm on my way tuh see Bainter. Jest ride along with me. I ain't got a chance without a gun. Yuh kin take the Winchester. If Hoot Bainter doesn't vouch for me, yuh can swing me from any tree yuh got handy. But I want tuh talk tuh Bainter before I say any more."

"Yuh ain't sayin' enough!" shouted a cowboy.

"Maybe. But maybe there's facts that I can't tell—'xcept to the law."

"I'll ride with yuh to Toughgrass," said Jack Bantley, doggedly. "That's the law—tuh give every man a chance to talk."

"We're givin' him a chance tuh talk, but he ain't sayin' much!" bawled a cowboy.

"He's jest a nacherally tricky hombre!" bawled another man in a rage. "Yuh cain't tell me he ain't thinking out some trick. I know these hellions. Say, this feller might ha' bin with the mob that kidnapped Miss Linda! What d'yuh know about that?"

Everything was looking pretty grim. Ben Harvey tried to shout some sense into the enraged waddies, but he could not make himself heard. He knew how explosive these cowpokes were with their deep hate of lawless men often overruling their judgement.

Jack Bantley was looking grim, too. He knew what was in the minds of the cowboys. And then, suddenly, a lariat whipped out and bound Ben's arms to his side. A rider on a big gelding backed his horse, tugging Ben forward.

Ben struggled for his guns, but his arms were bound tight by the lower part of his elbows. True, he could touch the tops of his holsters, but he could not whip a gun out.

Even so a drawn gun would have sealed his fate. They would shoot him down, convinced that a man who went for his guns was guilty.

The rider on the big gelding was dragging Ben and his horse to the clump of cottonwoods. All around the cowboys shouted and argued, some for the hanging and some against. Jack Bantley was worried, and he knew he could not control some of the angry punchers. Linda Harper's face was bloodless now, but she had not relented even though there was dawning horror in her eyes.

"Yuh damned fools, yuh can't hang me!" shouted Ben. "I demand some feller go git Sheriff Bainter!"

There was a confused medley of shouts and angry retorts as the men argued among themselves.

But all the time, the group drew nearer to the big cottonwoods, with the hot-headed rannigan determined to whip the lariat over a branch.

That was the quick drop to boothill—a lariat tightened round a sturdy branch—a horse that is suddenly slapped out from under the rider—a dangling figure that first jerks like a madman and then gradually becomes still as the noose tightens.

It was a horrible picture that came into Ben's mind. He had seen it happen before—mostly justifiably—and he had never lost his horror of the whole business. Now, maybe, it was going to happen to him. Was he going out this way?

Then Jack Bantley made his last appeal.

"Lissen, men. Yuh got to give this hombre a hearing. Hitch him up, if yuh like, but be mighty careful. I'll ride sweat out of this cayuse of mine into Toughgrass to rout out Hoot Bainter an' bring him out here," he looked around him at their angry faces. "Yuh got to wait, though. Miss Linda, say yuh'll stay and see fair play."

"He's a tricky galoot!" shouted a man.

"Hang him high! He's a Stangle's man!"

Linda Harper raised her hand suddenly. She stared at Ben with cold, grim eyes. He stared back, as if challenging her judgment and something in his expression made her turn her head quickly.

"I'll stay here, Jack. Ride into Toughgrass and get Hoot Bainter out here quick. The quicker the better."

"Yuh'll see these rannies don't do anythin' they might regret later on?"

"This man will still be alive when you come out with Sheriff Bainter," said Linda, coldly. "But I don't believe he is anythin' but a lowdown skunk—a member of a gang who'd kill an old man for his gold. Ride out, Jack."

Jack Bantley nodded in relief. As he wheeled his horse to go he shouted, "I figure he's an outlaw myself, but we got tuh stick tuh a fair hearing!" And then his horse was galloping away, the thunder of its hoofs diminishing in the distance.

Ben said, mockingly, "Thanks, ma'am. Yuh saved my life—so far."

The punchers fell silent, staring at Ben grimly. There was no relenting in their faces, and even those who had been for a fair hearing were now content to wait. The only exception was the hothead known as Hank Topliss, and he muttered under his breath continuously.

Ben wished the thing was settled. He felt impatient. He wanted to get on the trail to Jed Stangle's hideout. But he had to sit on his horse, arms bound to his sides.

For perhaps ten long minutes the group sat, and the only motion was caused by the impatient horses as they tossed heads and pawed the ground.

Then came the thunder of fast riding horses!

All heads turned in surprise. The fast riding horses were coming from Palermo!

There was only the oncoming rumble of hoofs until a band of men swung into view round the large clump of cottonwoods.

Then there were gasps, snarls, pistol shots and a sudden crow-hopping of horses as the cowboys swung their mounts to face the oncoming men.

For the thundering charge was headed by Jeff Muldoon! There were nearly ten men, and they rode round the cottonwoods in a single file of madly galloping horses and spitting Colts!

Ben swore grimly. The band were not Stangle's men as far as he knew. There could be only one explanation. Muldoon had got word that Ben was trapped near the Flying T and had collected a band of desperadoes. No doubt Stangle would pay them.

It seemed Muldoon had got his skin full of whiskey!

Ben swore again. Everything looked like being an unholy mix up! Somebody would have to straighten the whole thing out—and quick!

Lead whammed into the trunks of the cottonwoods. A cowboy went down, spun round by a heavy slug, blood spurting from a stomach wound. Hank Topliss tried to jerk at the lariat binding Ben as if determined to hang the man.

Ben reacted as the noose slipped up his arms towards his throat. Hank was quickly twisting the rope so that it would tighten under his neck. But Ben Harvey knew a trick or two. He threw his arms up suddenly as the noose slipped up. He just beat Hank's savage tug. Instead of the rope tightening on his neck, the noose widened under Ben's outward moving arms. Ben ducked swiftly and the noose slipped over his head. It nearly tangled on his arms, but he threw it clear. Everything happened in seconds.

Ben knew instinctively he had to get away from the Flying T cowboys because they would turn and shoot him as soon as they recovered from the surprise of the attack. In theory he was with the punchers against the murderous desperadoes, but the cowboys did not know that! It was no good arguing with bullets! He had to get away and quick. Explanations would come later.

All such thoughts flashed through his mind in seconds, and simultaneously he whirled his horse. His bay blundered against Hank's cayuse and the cowboy's mount reared. Hank Topliss was nearly unseated and he grabbed the reins with both hands. As the puncher fought his spooked horse, Ben rowelled his cayuse. The big bay leaped forward and galloped out of the cottonwood clump at a terrific speed.

Ben crouched low in the saddle, felt singing lead flying past his head. He had a rotten feeling that any moment a slug would bite into his back, for lead was being exchanged all ways. With his head low on the horse's neck, he saw little of the gunplay in the tense flight of seconds that bore him out of Colt range.

Then he straightened up, jerked his horse round so that he could view the cottonwood clump. Now that he could see the whole scene, he did not like it. Three cowboys had evidently gone down in the first surprise shots, and there were only four left against about nine desperadoes from Palermo. Moreover, the men in the cottonwood clump were a stationary target, even though they had cover. In addition the Palermo men had ridden into the trees and were chasing the out-numbered punchers from one cover to another.

Ben thinned his lips grimly. He withdrew his guns. He could not stand by and see men killed by desperadoes. He would have to pick off the Palermo men in spite of his desire to keep in with Stangle's gang.

He spurred his horse, and the bay sprang forward. He was about to shoot at an attacker when a rider rowelled his bronc furiously out of the cottonwood clump.

The fleeing rider carried Linda Harper across his saddle!

It was Jeff Muldoon carrying the struggling girl away from the Flying T men. Apparently he had ridden into the scattered group and picked the girl from her horse.

As he spurred his horse into furious strides, Jeff shouted the men to withdraw.

"Git out! Cover my rear, yuh hombres!"

His bawl was audible to Harvey. As Ben's big bay cantered closer, he was caught in the fast riding group of Palermo desperadoes as they charged out of the trees. Jeff Muldoon saw Ben and beckoned with a smoking gun.

Ben rode out with them, and lead sang after their retreating backs. The Flying T men were collecting their horses he saw as he flung a backwards glance. They intended to give chase.

Ben figured the set-up in quick, savage thoughts. He could and he would shoot Jeff Muldoon down sooner than let Stangle get the girl, but was it advisable right now? If he shot Muldoon he would get a slug in the back himself. That was not his chief worry. If he got a bullet in his back he could not guarantee that another desperado might not pick the girl from Muldoon and get her to Jed Stangle. Already the Palermo band had a head start, and they might turn and form a cover in the hills, allowing one rider to get away to Stangle's hideout.

So whether he liked it or not he was riding with the outlaw band!

Jeff Muldoon was a big man and he kept hold of the girl fairly easily as his horse thundered over the prairie. The pounding band of ruffians rowelled their horses on to the trail to Palermo, with the re-formed group of Flying T men urging wide-eyed mounts in pursuit. A few shots rang out, but the range was now too great for the punchers. Indeed they were far behind, and Ben thought they would not make up the lost headway.

The rapid tattoo of hoofbeats continued for a mile or more of the Palermo trail, and then the whole bunch of desperadoes swung off into the first of the foothills. Jeff Muldoon was leading all the way, cruelly spurring his horse in spite of the double burden. The renegades from Palermo swung with Muldoon and Ben Harvey into the hills although their usual haunts were in the outlaw town.

Ben wondered how the news of his capture by the Flying T men had got to Palermo so quickly, but he had the vague impression someone must have seen the events under the cottonwood clump and rowelled a cayuse back to Palermo.

In another flash of thought he wondered what Jack Bantley and Sheriff Bainter would think when they got to the cottonwood clump on the borders of the Flying T spread—but perhaps they had heard the shooting. Certainly they would see the dead punchers.

The low foothills became more rugged. Ben

recognised the trail as leading across the fast trail to Jacknife Hill. But that ride would take some time, and long before that some of Stangle's hirelings would make a stand to allow Jeff to get the girl away. They could cover up behind rocky outcrops and coulees, exchange lead and then, after some time, slip away, one by one, in all directions. The Flying T men would not find the trail that led into Jacknife Hill because it was not too well-defined and crossed by numerous deer trails.

So the set-up was pretty good for Stangle's hirelings. No doubt they thought they would benefit when Stangle got the Guadalupe gold.

But they were reckoning without Ben Harvey, Texas Ranger!

"Not that yuh're in such a nice spot, old son," he muttered to himself. "Yuh can't go to the Flying T hombres 'cause they'd fill yuh full of lead. An' yuh can't shoot Muldoon and git the gal away jest yet 'cause these hellions would chop yuh guts up with Colt lead and still git Linda Harper to Stangle!"

His best bet was to lie low and stick to Jeff Muldoon. He had a plan already in his mind and felt pretty confident in spite of the fact that his scheme to hand Muldoon over to Hoot

Bainter and ride a posse up to Jacknife Hill had misfired.

It was still possible to get a posse up to the hideout and shoot the hellions out of their eyrie! But he would have to work fast!

As Ben had thought, the band of gunnies chose a bottle-necked ravine to make a stand which would delay the pursuit. It was shale, rock and clay terrain without more than an occasional scrub cactus to afford vegetation for a few jack-rabbits. The men swiftly corralled the horses in a natural corner, and then took up safe positions among the numerous crevices. Jeff Muldoon roared to Ben, "Yuh needn't stay. Stangle expects yuh back."

Ben nodded and urged his panting horse up the steep shale incline. He was listening grimly for the first shot. He hated thinking about courageous men riding into that trap, but there was nothing he could do. Anyway, the Flying T men might give as good as they received.

He was quite aware that he could shoot Muldoon now and ride the girl back to her ranch by a roundabout trail. But the news would reach Stangle. Muldoon would be found dead. The Palermo men would know Muldoon had ridden off with his pardner. Stangle would guess he had been tricked, and the worst of it was he still had Tom Wilson, Linda's stepfather.

Suddenly Ben shouted to Jeff Muldoon.

"I'll catch up with yuh. I reckon I oughta give those hombres a hand against those Flying T fellers. They had me all ready to string up!"

Jeff Muldoon snarled savagely. "Yuh needn't go back. My hoss can't take this double load all the way at full gallop. Yuh'll have to take this gal on that big bay soon."

Ben nodded but inwardly he felt grim. His sudden idea had been to get among the rocks and pick off one or two Palermo men. He would have felt better. But he could not arouse Muldoon's suspicions by going against the other man.

Their horses slithered down the shale on the other side of the ridge. They found a rideable ledge that took them across flat slab rock, and in the distance they could see the trail where it entered a rocky defile. The sun was brassy and intense, a burning orb that made their saddles smell of hot leather.

Muldoon spurred his horse through gulch and sandy draw until the animal was lathered. He kept a brawny arm round Linda, for she never stopped struggling. Eventually the breed halted his horse and snarled to Ben.

"Take this gal offen me! My hoss is plumb tuckered, but I'll git along without the gal."

Linda was handed over to Ben not without further struggles. Ben held her with one arm, his face grim, his wits racing. She beat at him with her fists, and he had to take it. He spurred his bay down to the trail and kept up a steady lope while Linda fought his retaining arm. Behind him Jeff Muldoon grinned savagely.

"You lowdown skunk!" panted Linda. "The boys should've put that noose round your neck there and then and that would've been the end of you!"

"Shore would have," agreed Ben, sombrely. "But I don't reckon tuh die that way."

"It'll be that way or lead!"

"Maybe. I've had my share o' lead dodgin'."

He wondered if Jeff could hear her rapped comments, for he was riding close enough.

"I hope I get the chance to kill you!" snapped the girl again.

"Yuh might git the chance," retorted Ben, "but I hope yuh can't aim too well."

"I can aim pretty good!"

He felt some macabre humour in the hate the

girl so obviously felt for him. He held her by the waist, holding down one arm while he dodged the blows she tried to rain with her other fist. How she hated him, and he had only admiration for her!

Then suddenly he sickened of the whole plan he had evolved. It was too risky taking Linda Harper to Stangle's stronghold even if he had plans to smash the outlaws with one quick blow.

"Listen," he said. "I'm not with Jed Stangle, no matter what yuh think. I can't expain more —Muldoon might hear, though I don't think so. But I don't want to let him even see me talking much to yuh. I'm going tuh set yuh down. Don't run off. Jest trust me. Don't run off—yuh couldn't git far in these hills without a hoss. I aim tuh git yuh a hoss. Now!"

The trail was pretty flat and they were a long way from the ravine where the Palermo men were holding up the Flying T men.

Ben suddenly lowered the girl to the ground and skidded his horse to a stop in one motion.

Jeff Muldoon was at that moment some three yards behind him and he nearly blundered into Ben's horse. Ben dismounted and walked away from the girl. He wanted to get well away from her.

"What yuh stopping for?" shouted Muldoon. "Git that gal up on that hoss. Stangle wants her!"

Ben turned, stared at the breed from a distance of ten yards. His grim gaze brought a flood of doubt to Muldoon's face.

"Stangle ain't goin' tuh get the girl," said Ben, briefly.

The breed looked at him suspiciously.

"What the hell d'yuh mean?"

"What I say, Muldoon." Ben paused deliberately. "I'm agin yuh, Muldoon."

"Yuh mean—?"

Fear chased over the outlaw's sallow face. He sat his saddle as if tensed for battle.

"I'm giving yuh fair warning," said Ben, sombrely.

He paused again. Muldoon sat his saddle completely motionless. Ben stared back with narrow eyes. The breed knew now what he meant. There was no retreating for either of them. Within a few seconds one of them would go for a gun.

The outlaw sat and sweated and then cursed.

"Yuh durned—Yuh're a double-crossing

polecat. Yuh're a dirty—" He mentioned an unmentionable name.

"Yuh've got a chance," said Ben, thinly. "Take it, hombre. Or maybe I'll have tuh gun yuh where yuh sit."

"Stangle will kill yuh, yuh blasted—!"

And then Muldoon's hands flicked for his guns. The two Colts swung up with incredible speed. The breed was a gunman of long experience and many fights in gunsmoke.

Crack! Crack!

Two shots barked across the trail simultaneously. Ben's hands flew with grim speed. He had recognised Muldoon as a quick gunman, and he just had to beat him even though he gave him a split-second on the draw.

Ben's Colt roared—and the slug took Muldoon between the eyes as he sat his horse.

Ben felt a slug tug at his sleeve at the top of his left shoulder. Muldoon had aimed for his heart and missed!

The breed had been too quick and his shot had veered. Ben stood with smoking Colt while Muldoon toppled from his horse.

The man hit the ground and the bronc jibbed at the gunplay. Ben went over and grabbed the reins. He looked up to Linda Harper and said sombrely, "I gave him a chance. If he'd got me, Stangle would've got yuh, and Gawd help yuh after that. Even so I had to give the hombre a chance."

"Yuh shot your own pardner!" gasped Linda.

"I've told yuh I'm not working for Stangle. I'm trying tuh help yuh. Understand?"

She looked helpless for a second.

"Won't Stangle suspect you? Won't he get to hear you've killed this man?"

"I've got a story to tell Stangle," said Ben with a trace of humour in his voice. "Now git on that horse. We've got to move fast. Maybe those hellions will ride this way after they sling some lead at the Flying T hombres, and maybe they won't. But we got tuh get ridin' fast."

He helped her get Muldoon's bronc and adjusted the stirrups quickly. Within seconds they had wheeled both horses round and were heading down the trail that would lead through a tangle of foothills past Palermo.

6

Pay-Dirt Plan

LONG before they came to the foothills she was firing questions at him. Linda's curiosity was aroused.

"You're not an outlaw!" she accused.

"Nope," he said briefly.

He was wondering just how much to tell her. He had a great urge to clear himself in her eyes, and make himself respectable. He could tell about his great record in the Rangers, and the assignment he had been given. But was it wise?

So far only Sheriff Bainter knew his true identity, and most of the Flying T men would definitely think he was an outlaw. In their eyes he had staged hold-ups in Toughgrass, gone in with Stangle and now shot his way out of a necktie party with the aid of Palermo ruffians. He was in bad, as far as the respectable community of Toughgrass was involved.

But Jack Bantley had dashed off for Sheriff Hoot Bainter and maybe by now the sheriff had told Bantley a few things about the man they had intended to hang. Bantley would have to believe Sheriff Bainter, in spite of the dead men they would see under the cottonwood clump on the Flying T spread.

So that meant Jack Bantley was in on the secret of his identity and his mission in this territory. And Linda Harper would suspect he was not the outlaw he appeared to be.

"You actually joined up with Jed Stangle?" she asked, as they rode down the trail.

"I joined up," he said.

"Why?"

"I think I gave yuh a hint—to rescue yore step-dad, Tom Wilson."

"There's some mystery about you," she challenged.

He looked worried.

"Look, Linda, I can see yuh're pretty curious, an' I figure yuh'll be asking Hoot Bainter questions when yuh get back to Tough-grass. So I might as well tell yuh everything now. But I want yuh to promise to keep it a dead secret—as I know yuh will."

"I promise—if it's to help my step-father," she said, quietly.

"It shore is. Wal, my name is Ben Harvey,

and I don't come from these parts—I'm from the east. I'm a Texas Ranger."

She stared in increasing wonder.

"A Ranger! Oh, I thought you were some sort of outlaw who was trying to reform—help Sheriff Bainter—or something like that—"

Her voice trailed off.

"No, ma'am. I'll show yuh my star."

He fumbled in his belt, taking the badge from his secret pocket. He felt a great desire to establish himself in her eyes.

She stared with dawning admiration at the silver badge he held out to her. She took it in her hand, scrutinised it for a few seconds and then handed it back to him. He put it away very carefully.

"So yuh see, I've got the job of getting yore step-dad from Jed Stangle," he said slowly. "I was sent out here by Captain MacAdam, Commanding Company 'B', Texas Rangers, from Fort Amigo."

"What about the hold-ups in Toughgrass?" she asked.

"Just a blind."

"And they got you in with Jed Stangle?"

"Shore. I had a fight with his *segundo*. He hates me."

"You know Stangle's men kidnapped me from the ranch?" she questioned.

He grinned.

"Shore do."

"What are you smiling about?" she demanded.

The horses picked a way at a steady pace down the wandering deer trails. Ben kept an eye open all the time.

"I wasn't really smiling," he said.

But she had a quick intuition.

"I think I begin to understand. I asked Hoot Bainter how he got me away from Stangle's camp and he was very evasive. Said something about a deputy—but no one knew this deputy. Not even Jack Bantley when I asked him. The deputy was you!"

He nodded his admission.

"Yeah. I had to help. I was at Bainter's place when a rider came in with the news. I rode out with Hoot Bainter. We found Stangle's men camped on the trail."

"Who actually got me away?"

Ben shifted uncomfortably in his saddle.

"I reckon I actually picked yuh outa the place, but—"

"I wondered. The last I remembered was that hombre hitting me."

"He'll be a dead hombre someday," said Ben, grimly.

"And to think of the things I just said to you!"

"Jest forget it, ma'am."

"But I said some awful things—"

"Yuh really thought I was a murderer and an outlaw. Yuh said everythin' yuh were entitled to say at the time."

"And those waddies might have hanged you!"

Her eyes were wide now. Ben smiled assurance at her, as the horses brought them nearer to the trail leading to Toughgrass.

"Shore might, Miss Linda. I reckon that was a nasty moment."

She swallowed, as if the recollection of the scene under the cottonwoods was difficult to think about.

"It might have been terrible."

"It might, but it wasn't. Jest forget that, too."

"I have a lot of things to forget." She smiled at him. "Most of all the rotten things I said to you."

"Now that's all over. Yuh can start on a right foot now, I reckon."

"When will you get Tom Wilson away from Stangle? Won't it be dangerous for you?"

"Yeah, it might, but I jest got to take chances. I'm in Stangle's confidence, an' that's something. But Rocky Creel shore hates me. I'll have to watch that hombre."

"Who is Rocky Creel?"

"The *segundo* I told yuh about."

"He's the one who hates you." She caught her breath, and made a little instinctive gesture with her hand. "You'll have to be careful."

"I'll be careful, Linda," he said, slowly. He looked up at her with a gleam in his grey eyes. "From now on I'll be careful."

There was something in his voice and she did not fail to catch his meaning.

"But not too careful," he added with a grin, "so that those hellions get away with their crimes."

She turned her head away.

"I can't thank you enough. You've rescued me twice from Jed Stangle. He'd do anything to get the secret of my father's gold mine."

"Yeah. We haven't got to overplay our

hand," he muttered. "He's a mighty tricky hombre."

They were nearly at the parting of the trails. He halted his bay, and she turned Muldoon's bronc so that she was facing him.

"This is where we part," he said slowly. "Now I want yuh to ride quickly to yore ranch. See Jack Bantley. Maybe he has talked with Hoot Bainter. If he hasn't, yuh can git to Hoot Bainter and tell him I reckon to light a mighty big fire in the hills tonight. Tell him Stangle's hideout is in the Jacknife Hill. Tell Hoot Bainter to git a posse—a big one—and ride up into them hills. I'll give him time to git up there, and then I'll light a fire."

"But how will you do that?"

"I haven't worked out the details yet, but I've got the general idea. Naturally, I'll have to go against Stangle. I figure to git Tom Wilson and barricade myself in one o' those caves which is mighty full of merchandise and guns. Then I'll git a fire going, and that'll lead Hoot Bainter and his posse to the hideout."

"If anything goes wrong—" she began.

He said grimly, "It won't have tuh go wrong. But if it did, I'd be in a pretty fix. Kinda like some other situations I bin in."

"You been in fixes like that before?" she gasped.

He looked in surprise at her amazement.

"Wal, pretty much the same. Now yuh got the idea right in yore mind?"

"Yes. I have to see Jack Bantley and Hoot Bainter and tell them what you have in mind. You're going to light a fire in Stangle's hideout to guide a posse. And you're going to get Tom somewhere safe."

"Yuh got in pat," he said. "Now rowel that cayuse and git down tuh safety. Yuh still got many a mile tuh go yet, but I can't go with yuh. I might be spotted by some wandering punchers and find myself back as the chief character in a hangnoose party."

"I wouldn't let that happen!" she flashed.

He grinned.

"I was jokin'. But I've got tuh play it safe. I've got tuh put a limit on the number of people who know I'm a Texas Ranger. It's mighty queer how rumours get around, and I don't want the slightest hint tuh reach Jed Stangle."

"Neither do I," she said quietly.

"If my plan comes off tonight, it might be the end o' Stangle and his owlhoots. The main thing is to git Tom Wilson to safety."

110

They both hesitated as if reluctant to part.

"Wal, I got to hit the trail," muttered Ben, and he fumbled with the reins.

"I'll go straight to Jack Bantley," she promised. "There'll be a posse in the hills tonight."

"Bantley's a fine feller," he muttered.

"He is," she agreed.

"Yuh think a lot o' him?"

"He's a great foreman," she laughed.

"Yeah. A straight feller." He hesitated. "Wal, I must git this cayuse back into those hills. Yuh'll tell Hoot Bainter that Muldoon is dead."

"I will," she said, with sombre memory of the gun-fight.

"Adios," he said.

"Be careful," she whispered.

And Ben Harvey rode back along the trail, conscious that there was not much cause for rivalry between him and Jack Bantley!

Ben rode as fast as the rough terrain would allow and the jagged crest of Jacknife Hill came nearer. He encountered no other riders in the hilly badlands. As he rode up the trail to Jacknife Hill he realised how hidden the hideout really was to those who did not know where to look.

Sweat and dust caked his orange-red shirt and yellow bandana. His low-crowned hat was streaked with grey dust. There was the smell of hot leather about his horse. He certainly looked as if he had ridden hard and long.

He rode his bay up the rocky ledge and entered the camp. The Mexican was still cooking, though no doubt it was another meal, and men lounged around. They knew he was coming. They did not stare much. Somewhere a hidden trail guard had passed the word. Jed Stangle stood at the cave mouth, hands hooked into his belt. He stared hard at Ben.

"Wal, you got the gal."

It was a statement and not a question. Then. "Where's Muldoon?" Jed Stangle's tone was sharp.

"He's dead," said Ben briefly.

"Yeah?" Stangle narrowed his eyes. "How come? Where's the gal? Yuh're supposed tuh have the gal. Where is she?"

Ben lurched a little as if absolutely tired out with riding.

"We were drygulched. They were riders outa Toughgrass. I can't figure how they got round

112

us. Must ha' taken a fast trail out of town. It was like this, Stangle—Jeff an' I had the gal. A bunch of rannigans from Palermo covered for us—"

"I know all that," snarled Stangle. "I got the whole story. Yuh don't mean tuh tell me yuh lost thet durned gal?"

"I'm trying tuh tell yuh that," said Ben.

"Gawd! Of all the blamed—" Stangle lost his usual cold calm. He stamped around for a moment. Ben eyed him warily. He was not going to take a fast bullet from the outlaw in his rage.

"Looky here," shouted Jed Stangle. "I got a rider come up from the Palermo bunch an' he told me yuh had the gal—yuh and Muldoon. The Palermo bunch covered up for yuh in the canyons. Now yuh got the blamed nerve tuh tell me yuh got drygulched. Hey! Shorty!"

Stangle turned and bellowed at a group of men who were eyeing the rumpus between their chief and Ben Harvey. A man came up quickly. He was a stocky fellow in dirty range clothes. He had one eye and a patch over the other.

"Did Muldoon and this hombre get away with that gal?" rapped Stangle, returning to his dangerous, wary manner.

"Shore did. We swapped lead wi' them Flying T fellers and this hombre rode off wi' Muldoon and the gal."

"Who was carrying the gal?"

"Reckon it was Muldoon, Stangle, 'sfar as I can remember."

Jed Stangle stood before Ben.

"I know all about the necktie party yuh ran into. Yuh can thank Muldoon fer gittin' yuh out o' that one. And now yuh say he's dead. I wanta hear all about it. Where did it happen?"

"Over in the east. Jest after we left the gunplay. A bunch o' hombres appeared from nowhere, and shot Muldoon to hell."

"How did yuh git away?"

"I jest kinda got behind some rock. I threw some lead, but it was hopeless. Muldoon was dead, and the gal had rolled clear o' his horse. The other jiggers had picked her up in a few seconds."

Stangle spat one word. "Tarnation!"

"Yuh worried about Muldoon?" asked Ben calmly.

"Nope. But I was all set tuh git that gal and make Wilson talk tonight. I wasn't gonna stand fer any fancy words, either. He'd talk or I'd

114

cut her to bits! Now, blast it, we're no further forward."

Stangle looked over Ben's head at the trail ahead.

"Maybe that hombre Rocky Creel has run into a heap o' trouble, too," he growled.

"Trouble? How come?" inquired Ben.

"He left with a pardner jest after you and Muldoon went down the fast trail. I figured yuh and Muldoon wouldn't know about it, but Rocky Creel and his sidekick were backing yuh up."

"Shore seems like it," said Ben, dryly. "Seeing I nearly got strung up on a cottonwood. Only Muldoon got me outa that jam. Where did Creel go?"

"That's what I'd like tuh know. Maybe he got bush-whacked like yuhself."

"Maybe," commented Ben.

"Yuh'd ha' bin glad of Rocky Creel if things had gone bad with yuh," grunted Stangle.

"Can't say things did go right," retorted Ben, "and this Creel hombre wasn't anywhere about. Why in hell didn't he get me outa that hang-noose party, if he was tailing me?"

Stangle shot him a sharp glance.

115

"Creel don't like yuh, hombre," he observed, briefly.

Ben rubbed his arms.

"Shore would like a mass o' beans and jerky. Yuh got some good beef here, Stangle?"

A brief smile flitted over the other's moustached lips.

"We got good beef."

"Right. I'm going to get me some," and Ben ambled past, leading his horse. Stangle watched him go thoughtfully.

Ben tended to the bay first, wiping him down, fetching him water. There was grass in a feed corral, and Ben led the horse to it. Then he took himself over to the Mexican cook.

As he squatted down away from the fire with a tin plate of grub he thought about Stangle's move in sending Rocky Creel to tail Muldoon and himself. Only Stangle knew his own exact intentions. Maybe he had not trusted Muldoon and him. Maybe he had genuinely thought Creel might be able to walk in and help as a last resort. But where had Creel been during the affair under the cottonwoods?

Probably Rocky Creel had known about that ambush Ben had ridden into, and figured it was a good idea to let him swing.

Ben shrugged. It did not matter now. The main thing was to figure out a method of getting Tom Wilson and himself barricaded in a cave with plenty of ammunition, rifles and grub. Then a fire would have to be lit, and not just a mere glow, but a veritable bonfire that would defy the outlaw's efforts to put it out. The fire would have to be fed so that it became a conflagration seen for miles around in the night. Sheriff Hoot Bainter and his posse would be in the vicinity of the Jacknife Hill hideout, and the flare-up would be the means of guiding them in.

Maybe they'd meet with lead spitting from all sides of the eyrie, but they were men who expected that. Stangle had to be beaten.

Ben sat with his back to a boulder and felt at ease. He was weighing up the layout of the camp. Stangle had not such a lot of men here. Maybe there were about twelve, with Rocky Creel and a partner still out. Still, fourteen men would take some prying out of a place like this.

He could see the corral, the main cave with the shack built inside in which Tom Wilson was kept prisoner. And there were other caves, including the one stacked with stores. That cave seemed to be the logical one to choose if he wanted to barricade himself and Tom Wilson inside it.

Ben wandered around after eating his fill. The grub had filled him and was not bad. The beef was undoutedly rustled, and the outlaws used only the best!

Ben exchanged words with one Mexican who lolled indolently against a tree, the evening sun sending its hot, slanting rays through the branches to the baked ground below.

"Stangle's kinda riled about losin' the gal again," he commented.

The other shrugged.

"So. Maybe we'll never go tuh them Guadalupes!"

"Yuh don't like the idea, hombre?"

The Mexican's eyes snapped.

"I do not say that. But—the Guadalupes—" He shrugged again.

Ben smiled a trifle grimly. The greaser was right. The Guadalupes was a terrible place. Stangle, of course, knew what he was taking on if he ventured into the foreboding badlands. The lure of gold was the thing that pulled men on.

Ben wandered on and began making talk with another man.

"Yuh got water here, pardner?" asked Ben.

"Shore. Gotta natural spring in one o' them caves."

"Which cave, pardner?"

"Thet little cave Stangle uses fer a supply store." The man stopped whittling with a hooked knife. "Like it here, stranger?" asked the man, slowly.

"Shore, if Stangle's gonna get some gold," replied Ben, promptly.

"He'll git the gold," said the man, again slowly.

"Yuh goin' into the Guadalupes wi' Stangle?" asked Ben.

"Yeh. Reckon I will. It's as good a way tuh bury me bones as any!" And the man began to laugh harshly.

"Ever bin in them badlands?" queried Ben.

"Bin in a place like 'em."

Ben looked round and then said casually, "The greaser there don't seem tuh like the idea o' looking for gold. Anybody else like that in this outfit?"

"Why d'yuh ask?"

"Guess I like tuh know how keen the hombres I work with are about any job," drawled Ben.

"Wal, thar's plenty hombres here willin' to

kill anybody if they can git their hands on Tom Wilson's gold—and that goes fer me, too! We'll go wi' Stangle soon as he gits that old buzzard atalkin' about that bonanza."

Ben nodded.

"Hope that's soon," he growled. "I'm gittin' gold fever, too."

The man laughed unmusically and attacked his stick again. Ben wandered on.

Stangle was evidently in his shack in the cave, for Ben had not seen him outside. Ben thought about going in to see Stangle again about future plans, and then he decided to leave the outlaw chief alone.

From his survey of the camp, he began to have high hopes for the night. Maybe before the night was out Stangle would be smashed and the old man rescued. The job would be done. For Texas Ranger, Ben Harvey, it would be time to move on.

Ben was standing at the top of the trail which lead down from the ledge, when he suddenly heard hoof-beats. They were slowly, plodding hoof-beats, as if two or more horses were approaching.

His mind cast round for a second, because he had to weigh up every little event now that he was in dangerous territory, and he decided it would be Rocky Creel and his sidekick returning. Ben thought he would stand by the trail and watch Rocky Creel pass.

It might be amusing to see the man's face! For Rocky Creel hated him. In a sense, therefore, Creel was dangerous.

Ben waited, lolling against a cedar. He could not see anything for the trail turned a sharp rocky bend only a few yards away. But horses were approaching as if walking after a long, hard ride.

And then the first bobbing head came round the bend. It was a dark-faced ruffian riding a steeldust gelding. A few seconds and the next horse appeared. Rocky Creel sat the animal arrogantly. The horse was carrying two. Ben stiffened in every suddenly taut muscle.

Rocky Creel's passenger was Linda Harper!

As the cavalcade of horses passed Ben, Rocky Creel glared mockingly at the man on foot. Ben stared and then grinned as if this was good news.

Linda did not look more than a second at Ben. Her face was pale, as if she had been

121

trying to stem tears. But she was obviously unafraid. Her spirit was unbroken.

Already the trail guard had sounded the alert, and Ben wheeled to see Jed Stangle standing at the cave mouth.

Ben could not understand what had happened. But pretty obviously something had gone wrong, that was grimly certain.

Linda was in Stangle's power in spite of his efforts! What had happened? How had Rocky Creel and his partner got hold of the girl?

Ben turned and walked after the horses. He reached a point on the ledge where Rocky Creel and the other man dismounted and brought Linda face to face with Jed Stangle.

"So yuh got her!" gloated Stangle.

"Yeah." Rocky Creel turned a sneering expression towards Ben. "Seems yuh had some trouble, hombre!"

"A little," drawled Ben. "Glad tuh see yuh got the gal, though."

"Is that so? Pretty ain't she? Maybe the old cuss will talk now. He's shore got reason tuh, now. Ha! Ha!"

Creel's discordant laughter grated on Ben's nerves, but he joined in with the other outlaw's raucous shouts of triumph.

"We got the gal!"

"Shore make thet catamount talk now!"

"Guess we'll git thet gold now!"

They were all jubilant. Even Ben slapped a greaser on the back, and the Mexican threw his smelly arms round Ben's shoulders. Even Stangle was smiling in cruel anticipation.

Linda, still in her buckskin jacket and skirt, faced them all with defiance, even though her face was white. She hardly looked at Ben, and he was grimly relieved to see she had her nerves under control. There were women—but not western women—who might have given vent to hysterics, screaming to him to do something. He knew, of course, that Linda would never go like that.

But how had Rocky Creel caught her?

Within a few minutes he heard the story as Jed Stangle began to ask questions.

"How'd yuh git her, Rocky?" Stangle shot out.

Rocky Creel grinned, his angular face cruel in its harsh lines.

"Heerd Harvey jest escaped a hangnoose party," drawled Rocky Creel. "Also heerd from some hombres in Palermo thet the gal was on the way tuh yuh, Stangle. Then, blame me, if

Brad and me didn't come across the gal ridin' down tuh Toughgrass by herself. She was using Muldoon's hoss."

"Muldoon's hoss!"

Jed Stangle threw a glance at Ben.

"Thought yuh said the gal was rescued by Toughgrass riders?"

"Shore was Toughgrass riders that dry-gulched Muldoon and me," drawled Ben.

"How come the gal was ridin' Muldoon's hoss?"

"How in tarnation should I know?" retorted Ben. "I told yuh I got out blamed quick, soon as I saw Muldoon was dead. Why don't yuh ask the gal a few questions, seeing yuh on the prod?"

"Shore will."

Stangle turned to Linda, his glittering eyes bright as an eagle's orbs.

"Who was the hombres shot Muldoon?"

"Toughgrass men," said Linda curtly.

"Just tuh keep in mind—which feller killed Muldoon?"

"I don't know, and I wouldn't tell you if I did."

Stangle permitted a thin grin to twist his lips.

"Yuh'll tell me plenty—ef I wanta make yuh.

Anyhow it don't matter—we got yuh here safe an' sound. We'll jest go along now and show yuh to yore step-dad. Maybe he'll see sense at last."

"Yu'd better not harm him—" cried Linda.

But only a chorus of raucous laughter greeted her words.

Ben joined in, turning away from the girl as if she was a matter of indifference to him. But Ben was aware of Rocky Creel's eyes. The man was suspicious of him.

The man could hardly have any definite grounds for suspecting him, and probably only disliked him, but Ben was well aware that the hangnoose party under the cottonwoods would afford any alert mind grounds for suspicion. For instance, if any of the outlaws got to hear that Ben had urged the would-be lynchers to send for the sheriff, they might wonder why Ben was so keen to see a lawman.

But for the moment he was safe. The outlaw band was cut off from Toughgrass and the rumours and comment. But if one hombre went into Palermo and heard everything about the rumpus under the cottonwoods, it might be bad business.

Linda was led along to the big cave by Jed

Stangle. Rocky Creel and a few other men came along, but some seemed satisfied to leave everything to Stangle. Ben went along, with the attitude of a man who was just plain curious. But he wanted to be near Linda. If anything happened, at least he had two guns which could play havoc.

They tramped into the shack built into the rocky side of the cave. On a rough bunk sat old Tom Wilson, his hands behind his back, tied. His bright old eyes glittered defiance at the outlaws, and then leaped to fires of despair when he saw the girl.

"They—they—they got yuh—Linda!"

"Don't tell them anything, Tom!" cried the girl.

The oldster groaned.

"But they got yuh, honey. I never figgered Stangle would git ahold o' yuh."

"Don't give in, Tom!" urged Linda. "I can stand anything they can do to me."

The old man groaned again.

"Shore, yuh got plenty o' spirit—jest like yuh Mother. How is she, Linda? Not aworrying too much, I hope!"

"She reckons yuh'll beat these pack rats somehow," snapped Linda, eyeing the outlaws.

But if she hoped to anger them, she was disappointed. Indeed Stangle seemed to be in a good mood, now that the girl was in his hands. He seemed to think it impossible that Tom Wilson should hold out on him much longer now.

And no doubt his views were right.

"We got plenty o' time," said Stangle almost genially. "We got all night tuh git information outa yuh, Wilson. If yuh got any sense, yuh'll give without us having tuh lay hands on this gal. Shore seems a shame tuh spoil her pretty looks." And Jed Stangle placed a horny hand under the girl's chin and jerked her head up.

Ben tightened little muscles inside his jaw. He wondered how much of this he was going to stand.

One thing was certain, he would not allow Stangle to lay a hand on the girl—at least beyond chin chuckling.

"But we want tuh git moving by sunup, Wilson," said Stangle and his voice hardened. "Git that into yore head—we start on the trail tuh yore gold in them Guadalupes by sunup. Everything is ready—hosses and grub. You and the gal go with us jest in case yuh figger tuh try a trick. Even ef yuh don't speak by sunup, we git moving jest the same. Yuh'll shore speak by the time we hit them Guadalupes."

"Yuh wouldn't take a gal into the badlands!" cried Tom Wilson.

"She'll go the best part o' the way," said Stangle. "Yuh could try foolin' us up to the last, Wilson. Until we sight that gold, the gal will be in our hands. It's the best weapon we got, especially when yore so almighty careless about yuh own health."

Tom Wilson's lips moved, but no sounds came. His face was still cut and bruised. His lips were cracked and dry as if the outlaws gave him little water.

Ben felt a great pity for the old-timer, but he dare not show it.

"We'll leave you two tuh have a good talk," said Stangle, turning to Rocky Creel. "And yuh can stay an' lissen, Creel."

And Jed Stangle rubbed his horny hands together with a rasping sound as he stamped from the shack with his followers. It seemed the outlaw chief was highly satisfied with events.

Ben would have liked to linger, but Stangle jerked his head indicating he had to follow.

Ben came out the cave with the men. Stangle said, "I want yuh to look over the stores and check the remuda. We got some good hosses, but I want yore opinion. We'll be mighty dependent on those hosses once we hit the badlands. Jest look things over an' let me know."

Ben nodded, and walked away. Stangle lounged down, his back to a tree.

Evidently Stangle still thought he was a hombre to trust! Ben had no delusions about his appearance. He was a big man and he wore two guns. He had a certain capable air. Stangle knew all that, and evidently figured he was a man to use.

That much was to the good. Ben was still not in a position to go against Stangle outright. For one thing he would have to get Tom Wilson and Linda to safety before any big move could be made. For another thing, Linda had evidently been unable to get to Sheriff Hoot Bainter. The sheriff knew nothing about Ben's proposed plan to light a guiding fire in the hideout, so it seemed that plan was useless.

Unless a posse was in the hills, it was useless to go on with the plan. To get Linda and Tom together and barricade themselves in a cave and light a bonfire was pointless unless a posse was coming to the rescue.

It was a bad setup, but he would have to wait for an opportunity.

He checked on the condition of the remuda. They were a good bunch of animals. Stangle would need them, especially the mules. Ben looked over the gear stacked in a little cave. There was plenty of food and spare saddle-gear. Everything was ready, stacked in neat heaps. Come sunup, there would be great activity in the camp. Men, horses and mules would set out on what was, in a certain sense, a hazardous expedition. It was more hazardous when one considered the hostility to each other of those taking part.

Looking at the packed gear, Ben's thoughts were busy. He wished now he had ridden down into Toughgrass with Linda. True if he had met up with Rocky Creel, there would have been a shooting match, and the outcome was anybody's guess. But he would have welcomed that. He was beginning to hate Creel even more than Stangle—if that was possible.

Ben walked slowly along the face of the rocky ledge that provided the caves. He could see Stangle with his back to a tree. Stangle had two other members of the owlhoot trail beside him, and they were playing cards. Stangle was a cool customer. He evidently thought there was no trouble coming his way, and that he may as well take it easy until sunup.

Ben sidled down the cave, towards the shack. He just had to see how Linda was faring. He certainly did not trust Rocky Creel.

As he came silently along the sandy floor, he heard voices from the shack. He recognised Rocky Creel's hard tones, and then Linda answering him coolly.

"Yore rannies nearly strung Harvey up in them cottonwoods," said Creel. "Too bad Muldoon interferred."

"You and Harvey and all yore ruffians have got it coming to you soon!" rapped Linda.

"How come yuh was ridin' alone down to Toughgrass?" demanded Rocky Creel.

"I've told you before—the Toughgrass men set me on the trail and then rode off to Palermo to try get some of the ruffians who rescued Harvey."

There was a moment's silence. Ben breathed in relief at Linda's answer. He could visualize Rocky Creel thinking deeply on this point. The man suspected something queer in the way he had found Linda riding alone to Toughgrass on Muldoon's horse. But Linda had provided him with a cast-iron answer, and he could not get to the truth.

Ben walked slowly to the doorless opening in the shack. He stood stock still.

"How come there was such a delay in hangin' Harvey on them cottonwoods?" pursued Rocky Creel.

"Some of the boys were against the lynching," said Linda steadily. Not for a second did her eyes betray the fact that she had seen Ben Harvey standing at the opening.

"Why?" asked Rocky Creel grimly.

"Because some are for law and order," retorted Linda. "That's why—if you can understand it! I don't get why you're so mighty anxious to see your pal hanged."

"He ain't no pal o' mine. Soon as bed down with a yellow-back. And I figger Stangle's a fool tuh trust him."

"Well, for your benefit, mister, I figure my rannies made a mistake in not hanging that hombre there and then," retorted Linda.

Rocky Creel eyed her narrowly.

Ben lounged into the shack, and Rocky Creel turned swiftly. He saw Ben standing over him, but Ben was smiling.

"Howdy, Creel. Yuh getting anything out the old cuss?"

Creel rose, hooked his fingers in his belt.

"Nope. Reckon that's Stangle's job."

"Figure we'll be on our way tuh that gold soon?"

"Shore. It's all lined up—but no thanks tuh you."

"Yuh figure I let them Toughgrass hombres git away with the gal too easily?" asked Ben as if in great surprise.

Rocky Creel showed his teeth.

"Nope. Maybe it was like yuh said—they was too many for yore guns."

Ben nodded.

"Shore that's the way it was. Sorry Muldoon had to get it."

Rocky Creel blinked his heavy lids.

"He was just a lazy breed."

"Yeah."

They stood eyeing each other, their real emotions hidden behind curt words. They both knew they hated each other, and that the barriers would break some day.

"Yuh want tuh get out in the daylight, Creel?" asked Ben.

"Why?"

"I'll keep watch on this gal for yuh—that's all."

"Right. I want tuh talk tuh Stangle, anyway. Remember, she's as clever as a coyote, Harvey. Don't let her get away from yuh."

There was more than a warning in the clipped words!

Creel walked out with clumping noises. He was a big, angular man and moved clumsily. Ben watched him through the rough "window" in the shack, and then he turned to Linda Harper.

"Are yuh all right, Linda?"

"Fine as I can be," she said, and her eyes gleamed with hope now that there were no outlaws to see them.

"We're not beaten yet," commented Ben grimly.

Tom Wilson stared with puzzled ears and then began to talk in a high-pitched cackle.

"What yuh say, young feller? Durn me ears! Did I hear yuh say we're not beaten?"

"That's right, old-timer," said Ben swiftly. "Linda will tell yuh everything later. Right now I want tuh say, don't worry. I'm gonna git yuh out o' here. How I don't rightly know, but I shore will. And jest to make it easy for yoreself,

134

give Stangle something to work on. Tell him something about the gold. Give him a location even if it's near to the bonanza."

"Are yuh workin' fer Stangle—" began the old-timer in a low growl of suspicion.

"He's a Texas Ranger," said Linda swiftly and quietly. "He nearly got me away from Stangle's men and it was just bad luck Creel caught me. Creel and his pardner seemed to appear from nowhere just after I left you, Ben."

"I'd like tuh shake yuh hand, son," said Tom Wilson gruffly. "But they got me tied, the pesky galoots! Durn me, cut these ropes an' we'll shoot a way outa this place!"

Ben shook his head regretfully.

"Yuh wouldn't get away with it. We ain't got horses ready. And I've only got two guns. Nope I want yuh to hang on, Tom. I want yuh to give Stangle some information so that he'll git that remuda o' his ready for sunup. Give him enough to work on and make it sound like yuh changed yore mind about keeping the bonanza secret. Then when I see things are getting ready for the trip to the badlands, I'll know what to do."

"Have yuh got a plan, Ben?" asked Linda eagerly.

He hesitated.

"It's not so much a plan as an intention. Yuh got to get outa here, that's all—you and Tom. And yuh got tuh get out tonight. If we leave everything till sunup, it'll be too late. We got tuh move tonight."

"How? Can yuh git me a gun?" cackled Tom Wilson.

"It all depends on horses," said Ben quickly. "I'll have to get my bay and two other cayuses ready so when we jump out everything is set. And I want to stampede Stangle's remuda so that they have some danged trouble following us."

Tom Wilson chuckled.

"Yuh got the right idees!"

"That's the danger," continued Ben. "Might be easy enough for us to git outa here during the night—especially when I got the run of the place—but if Stangle has horses to use in following us, it will be pretty dangerous."

"Yuh figger he knows all the trails?"

"Shore. So that's the plan. And for tonight. We get out o' this hideout. Too bad Sheriff Bainter won't be outside with a posse."

Tom Wilson was about to speak when Ben said, "Creel's coming back, old-timer."

Tom Wilson was a wily old fellow. He began to glare at Ben, and he was looking at the Texas Ranger as if he was poison when Creel stamped into the shack.

"Seen Stangle," grunted Creel. "He wants yuh, Harvey."

"What's proddin' him now?"

"Yuh'd better go an' see."

"Who's gonna look after the gal?"

"I kin do that nicely. I'm gonna tie her hands."

"In that case I'll wait for yuh. I take it yuh're coming out tuh see Stangle yoreself."

"Shore. Why not?"

Ben had to stand by and watch Rocky Creel tie the girl. As the man tightened rope round her wrists, he had the urge to smash the ruffian and fight a way out of the hideout—but he knew, even as he crushed the urge, that that was a fool-hardy impulse.

He even attempted to help Creel. The other eyed him narrowly for a moment, and then straightened.

"All right, Harvey. Let's go."

They tramped out, without a backward glance at the prisoners.

Ben wondered what was in Stangle's mind.

The outlaw leader was standing beside the tree when Ben and Rocky Creel tramped up. Jed Stangle was chipping wood with a large hack-knife. He looked up at Ben and Creel, narrowed his eyes and pushed back his hat. He folded the knife and put it in his vest pocket.

"Harvey, when I asked yuh to look the remuda over, I had an idea in mind. I want yuh and Creel to take the hosses down the trail tonight. It's slow work drivin' them, and I want to make speed at sunup. No point in startin' now for the whole camp, because the cayuses would hold us back."

Ben nodded.

"Yuh're figuring to make a quick start in the morning?"

"Yeah. A remuda is always hankering tuh stray, and that holds things up. You and Creel take them tonight and camp about ten miles away. Rocky will show yuh the best spot. We'll soon catch up with yuh tomorrow."

So Jed Stangle wanted the surplus unsaddled horses sent on in advance of his main party. It was a good idea—from his point of view. Loose horses often strayed, and time would be lost in rounding them up. The main band of outlaws would soon catch up on the remuda, and time

138

would be saved at the start, and it was unlikely that any of the horses left behind for the outlaws would go lame between now and sunup.

But would this spoil his plan to get Linda and Tom away from the hideout tonight?

Ben thought swiftly and decided it would not.

7

Hoglegs Of Hate

BEN HARVEY and Rocky Creel began almost at once on the job of driving the horses westwards on the first lap of the journey to the Guadalupes. A number of horses were left for the outlaws' needs and the prisoners, and the rest of the remuda led out of the corral.

Ben had decided to kill Creel that night.

He would set off with the horses, as Stangle desired, but they would not get very far on the long trail to the gold. For after a few miles there would have to be a showdown!

For Ben had determined to come back to the camp that night and get Linda and Tom away from Stangle. That plan still held good. Stangle's sudden decision had sealed Creel's death warrant!

Or had it? Was Creel a fast gun-man? At least he packed two guns, strapped low on this thighs, the butts shiny with use. Creel had killed before.

Stangle had evidently given thought to his remuda for the animals were in good condition. Maybe he had stolen most of them.

The horses came out snorting and crow-hopping. Creel took the lead with a big stallion roped to his saddle horn. The other cayuses followed with a tossing of manes, and Ben took up the rear. He was tired of riding, but this job had to be done. They set off to the accompaniment of roars and cheers from the assembled owl-hoots. The men had the idea that this was, at last, the start of their trek to gold. The remuda was off in advance. Before long the others would follow. And then gold!

Ben had no chance to speak to Linda. But she trusted him. She would follow his instructions, confident that he would devise plans to get them away from Stangle.

The evening sun was going down in a red rush to the horizon when Creel led the remuda down the trail. They were going westward, to the desert and then the hills where even rattlers found the parched heat too much. The Guadalupes, home of the magnificent eagle and slinking mountain lion, was tough country. It was waterless and arid in the valleys and plateaux, with only the mountain tops affording trees and water. And woe betide the man or beast that lost its way in those semi-desert regions.

But Stangle was not yet in the Guadalupes!

One thing was certain, Ben would never allow Linda to be taken along as hostage to that terrible country.

The beat of horses' hoofs on dusty ground was the only sound to come to Ben's ears for many a mile. Creel led the way, sure of the country. Ben certainly noted every detail for it was his habit to memorise every trail along which he travelled. The sun disappeared and twilight hovered strangely over the hill-land. In the scrub coyotes howled eeriely, and horses crowded together, wide-eyed and snorting.

Ben rode up to Creel from his position in the rear. He wanted to talk to the outlaw; there was no point in going much further.

Of course, it would have been easy to shoot the man in the back, but that was not Ben Harvey's code. Had they been anywhere near civilisation, he could have handed the man over to justice. But there was no justice in the hill country except that which a man carried in his guns.

All Ben could do was to offer Creel the chance to defend his life.

But first he had to talk.

"Say, Creel, how far to the spot we camp?"

The man turned on his horse.

"Another five miles. Are yuh lookin' after those cayuses at the back?"

"Shore. Creel, yuh don't like me, do yuh?"

Rocky Creel reined his horse, and the stallion behind cantered to a stop. The remuda slowed up behind the men as they reined in on the trail. There was scrub timber all around them, and the horses began to crop grass.

Creel knew instantly Ben was challenging him.

"Nope, I don't like yuh, hombre."

Ben sat still, his horse breathing easily.

"Yuh kin take it I don't like yuh, too, Creel," said Ben. "But for different reasons."

"Yeh? What reasons?"

"I'm not with Stangle, Creel."

Creel's bony face was a mass of shadows.

"Jest who the hell are yuh, Harvey?"

"I'm a Texas Ranger," said Ben grimly.

The other man stiffened. His hands steadied

in that peculiar motionless that precedes a wild clawing for the holster.

"Yuh—a durned—Ranger!"

"Yeah. Yuh know why I'm tellin' yuh, Creel."

"Reckon I do," said Creel.

They were slow curt words between two men, one of whom was going to die.

Ben watched for the other to move. He had a rigid code. The other man must reach for his gun first—but he intended the other man to die!

Creel said, "Yuh're a durned spy, Harvey. Yuh figger tuh kill me, huh?"

Ben did not nod. He said, "Shore" slowly.

Still Creel made no move.

"Yuh got just a few minutes, Creel," said Ben slowly.

"Maybe yuh the one with a few minutes."

"It could be."

Then Rocky Creel clawed savagely for his gun.

Ben slashed for his gun at the same time, and simultaneously his gun roared with Creel's.

Orange flame spat as lead sang out. Two guns roared death, but death came to only one man.

Creel slowly sagged sideways in the saddle as two horses reared wildly on hindlegs.

Ben slipped his gun back into holster. He climbed down from his bay and examined Creel, noting the slug had taken him between the eyes.

He had to find a spot where the vultures would not get the body. Outlaw or not, he was a man.

Ben wasted some time making a shallow grave and laying the body in it. There was an eerie light from a high riding moon, and it shone on the scene as he piled rocks above the grave. Creel had more done for him than Muldoon. But in that case they had been in a hurry to get to safety.

Ben took Creel's lariat and with his own he made a rope corral around the remuda. They were good horses and probably belonged to other owners than Jed Stangle; they would not stray out the rope corral that ran shoulder high round the scrub timber.

Ben rode away from the remuda conscious that he had started something which had not to fail. Because there would be no explaining this away to Stangle. If Linda and Tom were not rescued tonight, come sunup Stangle would head down the trail westward, and he would encounter the remuda—though probably some of the horses would be out of the rope corral. But Stangle would see enough.

Actually Stangle was going to learn enough before the night was through!

It was just that this was something Ben had not to fail in.

Ben rode back pretty steadily, taking a few anxious looks at the moon. He wished the moon would vanish, but he knew it would not. Whether he liked it or not the moon would shine its ghostly light on the hideout. He wondered if there was a trail guard posted during the night, and he decided there would be no guard. No one could find the hideout in semi-darkness. All the same, he intended to scout around.

He was in no hurry. Some of the outlaws might still be up, card playing or celebrating the start of their expedition. It might be a good idea if he entered the camp just before dawn when the men would be fast asleep.

By the time Ben got near to Stangle's headquarters, the night was well advanced in any case. There was work for him to do.

He spent some time going round the fringe

of the place like an Indian. There was, as far as he could see, not even a night guard in the camp. It seemed that Stangle was resting all his men.

Ben crouched behind a rock quite near to the place and tried a few coyote howls. He repeated the monotonous sounds for a few minutes just to see if anyone appeared. But they all seemed to be sleeping soundly. Stangle had faith in his well-concealed headquarters.

There were horses in the corral, and Ben intended to get two. He walked softly into the camp, keeping in the shadows but striding out to his objective. He reached the corral and let down the bars. He hoped none of the horses would whiney at his approach. As he led two out, he held his hand over the nostrils of one. But it was just temporary, for he had to lead two and he needed both his hands. The soft clop-clop of the horses did not arouse anyone in the camp. The corral was at the end of the ledge, for which fact Ben thanked his lucky star.

He had left the corral bars down. When he rode past again with Linda and Tom safely mounted, he intended to stampede the horses. With the corral bars down, they would gallop out quicker than a jack-rabbit. Had it not been for the necessity to get to the corral in any case, he might have brought back two spare horses from the remuda.

Getting horses was not going to be the worst part. Unless he was mistaken, the bulk of the men slept in the main cave on the sandy floor. And maybe some were bunked on the shack where Linda and Tom were kept.

Ben compressed his lips. If they got out of the hideout tonight without making a row, they would be lucky—in fact they would be lucky to get out at all.

He led the two unsaddled horses out to where he had left his bay. He would have to go back to the supply cave for saddles.

Ben walked softly into the camp again and went into the supply cave without disturbing a soul. It was pretty easy so far.

He carried the saddles back and fixed the horses up. He led them to a point right on the crest of the trail, and then he hitched the reins to a fallen log. They would be there when wanted.

As he walked quietly back into the camp for the third time, he took out his Colts. There would be no warning of his visit to any outlaw, but he would shoot his way out if needed.

Ben walked to the cave and halted. The moon scudded behind wispy clouds. So bright was the moon, the scant clouds could never veil it. Ben saw the first row of sleeping men as he sidled round a rocky face. He stood still, to see if his movements had been felt. Then he went a bit further into the cave. There was plenty of room to one side, and he went past sleeping men, step by step. He could hear their breathing, and once a man turned and mumbled in his sleep. Ben froze and stayed quiet for a minute, and then once again he went towards the dark outline of the shack.

He was not so sure what would happen on the return journey. It was ticklish enough by himself, but now he had to waken two persons and get them out—"

But perhaps Linda and Tom were awake, waiting for him!

He came to the rough shack and moved inch by inch to the doorway. He looked inside the gloomy interior and saw Jed Stangle sleeping on a bunk opposite where Linda and Tom had been placed.

Ben stepped softly inside the shack and

moved to the corner where Linda lay. Suddenly he saw a white face move and a voice whispered, "Ben!"

It was Linda and she was not asleep! Ben's knife slashed her bonds!

And then another voice whispered hoarsely, "Ben. You come, son!"

"Not another sound. Do as I say," Ben said in the lowest of whispers. "Move out with me, *but be quiet*!" And he cut more rope.

He handed Tom Wilson a gun he had picked up in the store. They all moved soft as mountain lions to the space which served as a door.

As they crept past Stangle's bunk, the outlaw stirred.

And then, as if with instinctive animal sense, he sat up swiftly, reaching for a gun.

But Ben was swifter. His Colt rammed Stangle's ribs.

"Make a sound and I'll kill yuh!" hissed Ben.

Stangle recognised him instantly.

"Yuh darned yellow-backed—"

"Yuh needn't say that again," hissed Ben. "There's a gal present. Git moving, Stangle."

With one hand, Ben took away the other's guns. He prodded with Colt, and Stangle got reluctantly to his feet.

150

"Yuh plump afraid to fire that gun," sneered Stangle. "Yuh'd have the whole camp on yuh in seconds."

"But yuh'd be dead," Ben said coldly. "Git moving, an' don't try any tricks. Hurry. I got hosses waiting."

"So yuh're a durned—spy!"

"Git moving!" hissed Ben.

His tone was enough to make Stangle move. The outlaw leader walked slowly to the shack exit. He was dressed even to his boots. Like many a follower of the owl-hoot trail, Stangle never undressed for months.

They began to move slowly up the sandy bed of the cave, and Jed Stangle was not attempting to move quietly. His boots clumbed with slushing sounds against sand and pebbles, and within a few seconds some of the outlaws had wakened with exclamations.

"Stangle! What the—"

"Jeeze! What's—"

Old Tom Wilson whipped round and began to back up the cave, his gun menacing the rows of sleeping men.

"The first galoot that moves gits a bullet?" he hissed.

Ben urged Stangle on. He raised his voice and

added his grim comment, "And Stangle will die pronto!"

Linda was in the lead, and if the tables were turned by some unexpected event, she would have the chance to flee for the horses.

In the white light of the moon, the party moved slowly and tensely to the cave mouth. Outside there was freedom, but as yet they were not free. The outlaws were watching every little move, and one might be tempted to throw a gun at Tom Wilson. The gallant old-timer was probably an experienced hand with a Colt and had the advantage of having his gun already out, but the light was bad and some man might risk a shot.

For Ben it was just a gamble. And to Jed Stangle his life was at stake. Even gold was not preferable to life.

Every yard brought them nearer to the cave mouth, and every second increased the tension. The only sounds were the slither of boots on sand and pebbles—and the hard breathing of Jed Stangle. And then they stood in the open. Ben beckoned to Old Tom Wilson, at the same time keeping one Colt fully trained unwaveringly on the cave.

"I want yuh to take this hombre, Tom," said

Ben. "Git down the trail and yuh'll find the hosses."

"An' what do I figger to do with this hellion?" barked the old-timer.

"Leave him. He's too much snakeroo for any straight hombre to handle."

"Should I shoot him?"

"If yuh feel thataway, Tom," said Ben slowly.

But Tom Wilson shook his head.

"Nope. Never shot a man in cold blood in my life and I don't reckon to start now. But ef he had a gun—"

"No time for that," said Ben swiftly.

Tom Wilson urged Stangle down the flat, rocky ledge towards the beginning of the marked trail. Linda went ahead to get the horses ready for an instant getaway. Ben moved back from the cave mouth because he realised he was in the moonlight and the outlaws in the gloom. Truth to tell, he was in a bad spot for sharpshooting, but so far the owl-hoots had not realised that.

He strode closer to the corral, still staring into the cave and holding twin Colts menacingly. Then he jumped behind a rock and loosened a rataplan of fire over the heads of the horses in the corral.

The cayuses broke out immediately, startled by the shooting. There were about little more than a dozen horses, and they streamed out of the opening in the corral and thundered down an ill-defined trail. They were successfully stampeded!

But the firing brought flashes of red from the cave. In the split second while Ben had fired towards the corral, some outlaws had leaped to advantage points, their guns spitting lead.

He felt the whine of several slugs as they passed overhead, and he flattened behind his rock and cursed. Things were not going just as he had planned, even though Tom and Linda were now with the horses and just about ready to get away.

But then plans had a habit of going astray, and so far the attempt to rescue the girl and her step-father was good enough.

But how was he to get away from this rock and join Linda and Old Tom?

All at once the bark of a single six-shooter from down the trail set up a new grim question in his mind.

Who was shooting? Was it Tom? Had he shot Jed Stangle after all?

There was no doubt that the shots came from that direction. Looking about him, Ben realised the first flush of dawn was not far away. The sun would come up rapidly, revealing a purply sky. But no matter—the outlaws' horses were stampeded, and it would take time to round them up and organise a pursuit. By then Ben hoped Linda and Tom would be well down the trail to Toughgrass.

But he had to find out about that shooting.

He looked around him. There was a series of boulders leading away to some scrub timber. He had to dash from boulder to boulder and risk the outlaws's fire.

Ben made the first dash without drawing a shot, but as he crouched low behind the boulder he realised the next dash would invite Colt lead. The hellions in the cave would guess his intentions. But he had to make it.

He came out, running and sprawling for the next boulder, and at the same time his guns spat viciously into the cave. He sprawled into the dust and huddled against rock and listened grimly as guns roared back at him and lead pinged into the ground all around him.

Hotter and hotter! The next dash would sure draw some trigger-happy hombres, but they might be deterred by the lead he would fling at them. At any rate, when he reached the next boulder he was well in the shade of the scrub timber and could move out instantly.

Ben waited until the hail of lead died down. He reloaded his Colts. Then he sprang for the other boulder, a running target for the men hidden in the shadows of the cave. But the light was uncertain and the range greater.

Colts roared and flashed orange flame. Lead stung dust from rocks and shale, and miraculously missed the plumetting man by inches. Ben showered hot slugs into the cave mouth— no mean trick while dashing like a hunted animal. He thought he heard a roar of pain, but everything was confusion. He was firing mainly to deter the outlaws and to keep them inside their cave.

He reached the rock and sprawled and tensed for a second. Then he leaped for the shadowy scrub timber that grew patchily on the fringe of the rocky ledge. He went dashing madly towards the spot where he had left the horses and where he expected to find Linda and Tom —if they had not ridden away.

Some of the owl-hoots had evidently left the cave as he entered the scrub timber, for he felt the hiss of lead as it followed him into the trees.

And then he was racing and slithering through shale, his boots digging furiously as he scrambled round a rocky outcrop at full speed.

He saw the horses and Linda mounted on one. She whipped round as he approached and gave a cry of relief.

"Where's Tom?" he panted as he ran up and grabbed his bay horse.

"Stangle got away from him, Ben!"

"Got away! Where's Tom now?"

"Stangle jumped Tom and got his gun from him. And then Stangle ran into the scrub and rock over there. Tom went after him. I heard shots. I hope Tom isn't hurt!"

Ben tightened his lips.

"I should have killed that snake. Linda, git that hoss down the trail. Here's a gun. I'll catch up."

"Where are you goin'?"

"I've got to see about Tom. I've got tuh find out where he is."

"Then I'm not goin' until you come with me," she said firmly. "And until we find Tom."

He gave her a swift stare.

157

"Linda—it's for yore own good—"

"Please—I'm in this, too. I can shoot—we've got to find Tom!"

He laughed grimly. He strode back up the trail a few steps, gun menacingly prominent.

"I'm agoin' to git Tom," he said curtly.

He hastened up and rounded a tall outcrop and then stopped and stared at the ledge with the cave in the background. Instantly he saw a group of figures and one man in the middle.

The man in the middle was struggling in the grip of Jed Stangle. Ben knew it was old Tom Wilson.

Stangle had partially reversed the situation, and Ben was grimly aware that to get Tom Wilson away now was pretty hopeless for one man. The outlaws were alert and gun-ready. They had the old ranch-owner.

But Ben took careful aim on Stangle and squeezed off a shot. The bullet hit the outlaw leader and he staggered, clasping his arm. Ben swore. He had missed a killing shot.

Then lead spat out towards him in a fury. Men unloaded guns at hard rock. Ben waited a second, realising he could not stay. They would surround him if he stayed, and they would kill him.

Stangle had Tom Wilson, and he knew Ben to be his enemy. It was a new situation.

Ben shouted at the top of his lungs.

"Hey! Stangle! Yuh got Tom Wilson, but I'll be back. Don't forget—I'll be back! I'm gonna kill yuh like I killed Rocky Creel and Muldoon. D'yuh hear me, Stangle?"

And he went swiftly back to where Linda held the horses. One leap and he was on the bay's back. Another second and they rode off in a thunder of hoofbeats.

8

Posse Pursuit

THERE was no time or opportunity for speech, and so Ben and Linda rode into Toughgrass at hell-for-leather pace, bringing sweating and dusty horses to a stop outside Sheriff Bainter's office. It was early morning and the sun was rising in its promise of torrid heat, and a few citizens of Toughgrass City were on the hard-baked street. One spotted Ben and raised a shout.

"That's the jigger who jined up wi' Stangle!"

"With Miss Linda, too!" another man bawled. "Wal, doggone me! What—"

But Ben had no time for them. Taking Linda along by the arm, he walked into Hoot Bainter's office, and the lawman rose from his desk to stare in surprise.

"Durn me if it ain't Ben Harvey—and Linda! Wal, am I glad tuh see yuh! We was jest thinkin' of getting a posse out in them hills today. Where's Tom?"

"We couldn't get him away," said Ben quietly, and he launched out on a swift tale of all the events since he had last seen Hoot Bainter. He told them about the hangnoose party and how Muldoon had got him away, and gave the sheriff the news that Muldoon and Creel were dead.

"Shore glad to hear thet," said the sheriff, his moustache bristling with satisfaction. He added, "But that hellion will git himself new *segundos*."

"Yuh heard about the hangnoose party?" grinned Ben.

"Shore. Jack Bantley got me tuh ride out tuh them cottonwoods, an' all we could see was dead Flying T boys. I had tuh tell Bantley about yuh—he was so mad wi' rage about yuh, Ben!"

"Bet he took a lot o' convincing!"

"He shore did. I had tuh show him papers from yore commanding officer."

Ben turned to Linda and impulsively held her arms. He looked deeply into her eyes.

"Yuh got to go on home an' just trust we get Tom Wilson away from Stangle."

She nodded. Courageous she might be, but trail riding in outlaw country was not for women who rode side-saddle! And Linda had the sense to know it. All the same, her eyes flashed.

"I wish I was a man! I'd be after Stangle—with two guns!"

"I guess yuh'd be after him with two guns if he came into Toughgrass," replied Ben. "But we're wastin' time." He tightened his grip slightly on her arms. "I'll be back, Linda. I figure to make myself look like a gentleman—get myself a new outfit maybe—and call on yuh."

"Yuh're a gentleman the way you are—trail dust and everything!" she said swiftly.

He grinned slowly and little realised she thought it attractive.

Then Ben turned to the work that lay ahead. He put an arm on Hoot Bainter's shoulder.

"I can show yuh Stangle's hideout. We gotta get a posse and get up into those hills—but fast."

"Ain't yuh had enough ridin' for twenty-four hours. Man, yuh bin at it since yuh rode into the hills to meet Stangle and then rode down to hit that hangnoose party!" Hoot Bainter chuckled richly. "Shore would ha' liked to see yuh sittin' under them cottonwoods wi' the noose round yore neck! What's it feel like, Ben?"

"Not so good," said Ben crisply.

The sheriff got to grips with the business on hand.

"Yeh. Wal, we gotta round up the posse. Miss Linda, yuh better git over to yore ranch, but yuh're not goin' alone. I got a deputy who lives along the street, an' he'll take yuh over. The deputy can tell Jack Bantley to saddle a hoss and git over here quick as can be."

And Hoot Bainter strode firmly to the door with the girl. He halted a second to rap to Ben, "Yuh had better git some rest. Maybe a wash would do yuh good!" And Hoot Bainter chuckled, for he firmly believed in his little jokes.

Ben grinned, too, and waved to Linda. As the girl went into the street with the sheriff, he watched from the window. He saw them ride off, and he turned away with a deep breath. Linda was safe, at least. Now to get old Tom Wilson.

He went out into the yard and sluiced himself with water. It was true—it revived him. He met Hoot Bainter's wife coming from the living quarters, and she promptly sat him down to a good meal.

Ben knew the posse could not be collected in seconds. It took time because some of the men were out on their daily work on the ranches. Maybe some would be miles away, but there would be plenty of volunteers. Toughgrass, priding itself upon its respectability and progress, did not like outlaws.

So there was time to clean himself up, and time to see that his bay had attention. He would need a fresh horse for the ride back to Stangle's hideout. The bay had had plenty of riding.

Of course Stangle would not be in the hideout when they reached the place, but the posse would have to ride there first to pick up the trail. It was Ben's bet that Jed Stangle would set off immediately for the Guadalupes, now that it was obvious that he could not get Linda Harper again. From the outlaw's viewpoint, it was still possible to make Tom Wilson divulge his secret, and get the bearings of the bonanza. But they would be risking Tom fooling them and losing the whole party in the terrible wastes.

Ben saw to a new horse in the livery stable next to the office. He gave orders to the man in charge to rest the bay. Then he went back to the sheriff's office, found some shaving tackle and began to scrape off his beard. As he shaved with the long-handled blade, men rode up, hitched their horses to the tie-rail and stamped into the office. Two came in together and nodded to Ben Harvey.

"Howdy, Harvey!"

"Howdy, strangers!"

"Hcard all about yuh from Bainter. He's ridin' round the town."

"Glad to hear that," said Ben, smiling.

"Heerd yuh're a Texas Ranger," grunted the other man.

Ben nodded, and went on shaving calmly.

At that moment another cowboy clumped into the office. He looked sheepishly at Ben.

"Say, I was in the party thet tried tuh string yuh up in those cottonwoods! I reckon I got to apologise. I jest heard how yuh got Miss Linda away from Stangle. I work for the Flying T."

"Don't need to say a word, feller," said Ben calmly.

But the cowboy walked round the room, shaking his head and muttering his own disgust of himself!

And then a newcomer strode into the office. It was Hank Topliss, the young hot-headed fellow who had been keen to hoist Ben on a branch of the cottonwood!

He looked even more sheepish than the other cowboy.

"Ain't I a doggone stupid idjut!" he addressed the room. "I wanted to hang a Texas Ranger! Say, Harvey, I'm goin' with yuh after them owl-hoots. They killed some pals o' mine in that rumpus under the cottonwoods."

"Yuh'll get yore chance," said Ben.

There were low growls from the assembled group. Evidently feeling against Jed Stangle was running high. And Hoot Bainter was certainly picking the right men!

And Sheriff Bainter was certainly telling Toughgrass all about Ben Harvey!

"Wonder that hombre doesn't git sick and tired o' tellin' the same yarn!" growled Ben.

He finished off his shaving and felt a lot better. He beat the dust from the orange shirt and grey vest he had picked out of Stangle's stores—and the black hat and yellow bandana. He checked his guns, and then made for the door.

"Time we were hittin' the trail," he said. "I'm agoin' for my fresh hoss and I want a saddle rifle."

166

He was in the livery when Sheriff Bainter rode up with a band of men numbering about ten.

"Linda Harper's back with her Mom on the ranch," he said.

Ben grunted.

"Thought yuh'd be interested," added Hoot Bainter, with the superior grin of an older man.

"Shore I'm interested. Thanks for the information," said Ben coolly.

"She's safe," reiterated Hoot Bainter with satisfaction.

"She'd better be after I got her outa that bandit hideout," said Ben dryly.

Then there was a swift motion to horses. The men were armed and carried hastily packed bags of food. None knew how long they would be in the hills, and a man had to eat.

The posse turned west into the hills just above Palermo Creek, and on their right they could see the shanty town of Palermo, with rattling buckboards and slowly moving Mexicans.

But the lawless town was not of interest, although there were many of Stangle's sympathisers there, and also many men who watched the posse as it swung west. The news would get around, as it always did.

So far Ben did not feel the strain, although he had been active and riding for the best part of the night. The heat was beating down again, and not a breath of air stirred. Maybe, as they climbed into the upland country, it might be cooler. Up in the mountains there was always a breeze.

He clamped his jaws whenever he thought of old Tom Wilson still in Stangle's grip. The outlaw would be furiously angry and capable of any cruelty. It was only because Tom had a valued secret, that the old-timer still lived. Once Stangle saw tangible evidence that the gold was to hand, old Tom would be snuffed out without compunction.

The posse was now in rocky, hilly country, with upthrusts of sandstone everywhere. They climbed the succession of shale ridges, with rock baked to sizzling point. They climbed higher, and then turned into a rocky canyon that turned in S fashion round the base of a large hill.

They were an hour out of Palermo and should not have been expecting attack, but the attack came nevertheless.

The attackers were a bunch of desperadoes from Palermo who had been contacted by a fast rider from that lawless town. The desperadoes had been out looking for a stage coach and were taking a short cut through the hills when the fast ride contacted them and told them the news of the posse riding out to exterminate Jed Stangle and his outfit.

The Palermo men had an interest in the continued existence of Stangle's gang, and a liking for gun-play. They were to get the gun-play!

But they chose the place, and the S-shaped canyon was perfect for a surprise bushwacker's attack.

The first intimation was when lead spat suddenly from the high walls of the canyon. Two men in the posse went down immediately their horses shot dead under them. The bigger target of the horses had received the bullets, and without horses the two men were useless.

Ben wheeled his mount and rode swiftly down to the struggling horses. He triggered fast bullets up at the vague outlines of men crouching behind rocky gullies in the high walls of the canyon wall. Men were shooting from all sides sending singing lead up to the canyon walls.

Ben turned his horse again, firing with his right hand Colt as he twisted in the saddle. The rest of the posse were feeding steel to their mounts to try to get away from the rataplan of lead. The two dismounted riders lay in the dust, bullet ridden by the desperadoes' guns. Beside them lay another body—but it had toppled down from the high walls of the canyon, spun from a safe spot by the force of Ben's bullet.

There were many curses and shouts—from all sides! Some of the Palermo outfit were hurt. But with the first surprise over, the Toughgrass posse were rowelling their horses. The cayuses leaped down the bed of the canyon, spooked by the gunfire and jabbed by steel spurs.

Ben urged his horse on, flinging a final shot with his right-hand Colt. He aimed at one of the ruffians standing up in a cleft of the rocks, and had the satisfaction of seeing the man jerk up his hands.

And then the posse were thrashing their mounts for dear life down the twisting canyon.

The desperadoes could not follow because they were positioned high above the canyon floor, and they had to climb down and find their horses. In any case, more than one had been hit and they were now anxious to make themselves scarce.

Ben rode his bay down the canyon with thundering hoofs, and came to the head of the posse again. He was glad to see Jack Bantley and Hoot Bainter had not been among the two men shot down nor were they injured.

"We ain't got time to ride back and shoot them out those clefts!" he shouted to the men. "Shore would like to, the danged hellions! But it would take too much time hunting 'em out. We gotta git on. Anyone who doesn't like the business can say what he thinks right now!"

But all that Ben heard was growls of anger, and he concluded that the men were all for the ride after Stangle.

The ride continued, taking precarious deer trails through the hilly country. Weary heat-baked miles went under fast clopping hoofs, and there was hot dust in the mouths of the riders and the smell of sizzling leather.

Miles slipped under thundering hoofs, with grim, silent men feeding steel to sweating cayuses. Through roughly gashed canyons and perilous shale slopes, they rode. Then there were fast stretches, but these were infrequent, though they took advantage of them. As they climbed higher they encountered timber, tall juniper and cedar but they were mostly isolated clumps, living on hidden moisture in the ground.

It was hard terrain even when they finally hit the fast trail to Jed Stangle's hideout. Here they made speed, because Ben had memorised the trail in all its tortuous turnings and criss-crossings with deer trails.

And then Jacknife Hill became a real hill instead of a purple haze on the horizon. As they rode nearer, the hilly slopes took on a definite form, the scrub timber and juniper clumps standing out.

Ben led the thundering posse right into the trail which dived and twisted through coulees in bewildering fashion. Dust and rock chips flew up under pulverising hoofs. The riders came thundering through to the rocky ledge where Stangle's caves lay.

There was no sudden whine of flying lead. The roar of Winchesters and Colts did not greet them. The posse spread out and dived for cover before the caves, but not a shot rang out.

Stangle had pulled out. The place was deserted.

Ben led the men through the caves, and they examined the remaining stores and loot. Stangle had gone in a hurry, but he had taken plenty of grub and weapons.

The whole place was empty and silent. The shack lay like a mute witness to the former activities of the place.

"Let's git on!" growled Ben.

"Maybe he'll cut yuh in if yuh ask him nice," he said.

"Maybe. We gotta git him outa Stangle's hands first!"

"We'll do it. Let's hit the trail, fellers."

Horses were wheeled, snorting and crow-hopping. The posse galloped out of the hidden ledge and went down the trail led by Ben Harvey.

He knew which direction Stangle had taken because the outlaw would go after his remuda. And there were the obvious tracks of hard-riding horses on the dusty trail. At this stage the merest tenderfoot could have read the sign.

Miles went under pounding hoofs. The territory was still barren and undulating, though occasional clumps of trees and scrub cactus were encountered. Ben knew there was one such large clump of trees where he had rope-corraled Stangle's remuda. That clump was their destination.

The sun climbed higher and was a red orb that stared down with hot breath at the sweltering earth. There was no water for the horses, but soon they would have to find it. The cayuses were lathered, and the riders white with dust, but there were water bottles for them.

Eventually the posse rode through the glade where Ben had roped the remuda, but the horses were gone. To one side lay the heap of stones that marked Creel's grave, and Ben silently indicated the spot to Hoot Bainter.

"Creel?" questioned the sheriff.

"Yeah. Satisfied?"

"Shore all the same to me," growled Hoot Bainter. "That hellion was a murderer."

"Let's keep movin'. I figure those hombres have a good head start on us."

"We'll git them if they're drivin' a remuda," muttered Sheriff Bainter.

"Shore will handicap them," commented Jack Bantley. "But they'd need those spare hosses for the Guadalupes."

"He's got more than hosses," said Ben. "He's got some mules."

"Shore hope they take a hankerin' to stop on the trail."

The three men laughed briefly, understanding the intractable nature of the mule as well as its stamina.

They entered wilder country, but the undulating slopes and small canyons were disappearing and huge canyons with high widely-separated walls dominated the scene. Ben figured there was probably fifty miles of this terrain before the desert proper came into view. This desert stretched for possibly a hundred miles in harsh, barren grimness before rising into the majestic and terrible Guadalupes.

But before long Stangle would have to make a stand.

All day they rode, and then towards evening they had their first exciting glimpse of their quarry. Miles away, like infinite specks, they saw dots moving slowly at the end of a huge canyon.

"Stangle!" said Ben briefly.

"Shore wouldn't be anyone else in this durned country!" grunted Hoot Bainter.

Breathing hard, aching in every limb, Ben

agreed. They had ridden hard, had not even stopped for a proper meal.

"Wal, we sighted 'em," he said.

"An' maybe Stangle's sighted us."

"We don't worry about that. That's him up there, an' he's got Tom Wilson wi' him. Yuh gotta figure on that, yuh fellers, before we start shootin'."

"What d'yuh mean, Ben? We'll shoot hell outa 'em!"

"Maybe," said Ben slowly, as he cantered his horse. "But don't forget we want to git Tom back alive."

Hoot Bainter spat dust.

"Yuh mean that ornery—"

"Shore. As yuh guess, Hoot. He'd think nothing of killin' Tom Wilson if he thought things were goin' against him. We don't want that."

"Shore don't."

"An' the only way to stop it is to git Tom away aforehand."

Jack Bantley was riding with Ben, and he glanced quickly at the Texas Ranger.

"That's a good idee. Yuh think we could—"

"Stangle will have to stop drivin' tonight— even if he plugs on until late after sundown," said Ben rapidly. "That's our chance. We've gotta be there when he makes camp, an' some feller has to git into that camp and git Tom Wilson out before the shootin' starts."

"That means we gotta make up the distance before he makes camp," said Sheriff Bainter.

"Yeah. We can't stop, an' the further Stangle drives after sundown, the more we gotta ride."

The pace of the horsemen quickened, even though weary mounts were hard put to respond to rowelling steel. The dots on the horizon, at the far end of the immense canyon, had disappeared, but they knew Stangle's outfit was just ahead, hidden by the contours of the land.

The ride went on, through canyon and valley. The harsh yellow rock and sand blinded the riders. They did not stop to eat, but munched meat and bread, hunched in their saddles. The distance between them and Stangle did not seem to diminish as hours slipped by, and it was obvious the outlaw had speeded up his gang. But the man would have to stop somewhere.

Twilight fell swiftly as the sun plunged below the horizon's rim, leaving the sky a mass of colours.

They were within the walls of a vast canyon,

and somewhere in that canyon Ben felt sure Jed Stangle had brought his men to camp. The night was quite dark, and warm air was still rising from the earth. Because it was too dark for men and horses, Ben was sure Stangle had stopped and was waiting for his pursuers.

The posse plodded on very slowly, Ben and Jack Bantley following the trail, crouching over their horses' manes, eyes peering at the ground. Now and then they had to swing down to get a close look at the sign. But all the time they were getting nearer to Stangle. He was somewhere along the line, in the canyon.

"Guess that hombre will be sitting pretty waitin' for us," grunted Jack Bantley.

"Shore to have a real nice spot," admitted Ben.

They went forward for perhaps another half-mile, and then Ben called a halt.

"Can yuh hear anything?" he asked of Jack and Hoot Bainter.

With the posse as quiet as was possible with tired, hard breathing horses, they stood in the darkness and listened. All around there was deep silence; the only noises came from the posse horses.

"I reckon somebody's gotta scout forward,"

said Ben softly. "We might walk into a bush-wacker's setup. Somewhere that hombre is just waitin' for us without a light and in dead silence. We've gotta locate him."

The others nodded.

"We'll go forward and spread out," said Ben. "Us three. If yuh hear or see anythin', come right back here. Then we can bring the whole posse up pretty close. Better tell the other rannigans that."

Ben, Jack and Hoot Bainter went among the men of the posse and told them the plans, then they set off, riding their horses slowly forward along the tracks left by the outlaws. Until they thought they were pretty close, they would stick together.

After some ten minutes of slow riding and peering for sign, they suddenly rode on to flat slab rock. They went forward for some yards, their horses' hoofs clanging on the rock, and they saw that the bed was likely to stretch for a long way.

"Looks like an old lava bed," said Ben softly. "Seen 'em before. Can't see much sign on flat rock. Can yuh, Hoot?"

"Nope. Those jiggers got the luck o' their breed. Figger we better spread out now, huh?"

"Yeah, spread out. If yuh sec or hear anything within ten minutes hit back to the posse. I reckon it best not to scout alone for too long. So we got ten or fifteen minutes on our own."

With that they moved off in different directions over the flat rock. Ben took a more central position, and began to lead his horse by the bit.

He soon found himself alone in the gloom, with nothing but his horse's hoofs making a dull sound on the rock. Try as he might, he could not find any sign on the hard rock. A dozen horses could have ridden that way for all the sign there was to be picked up.

So it was just blind guesswork. Stangle was somewhere in the dark canyon, but where?

Ben halted many times, listening intently. There was nothing, just brooding silence. He could not even hear sounds of Jack or Hoot. He would have to be careful he did not confuse them with the outlaws. And he hoped they would be careful, too.

The minutes were ticking by, and Ben was beginning to think Stangle had risked everything and gone on through the night, when he suddenly saw the movement before him.

He froze, halting his horse. He stood stock

still for a moment, wondering if he had wandered into Hoot or Jack Bantley.

He hobbled his horse with a rock weighing down the thrown-over reins, and he began to creep forward on his hands and knees. Although he could not see the figure again, he wanted to discover just what it was he had seen —or thought he had seen.

Within seconds he knew he had located Jed Stangle's encamped men. Ben crept up to a clump of cholla cactus and rock without making a single sound however minute. He sat and gradually saw the dim, shadowy figures that moved in the shallow basin in the rock. Stangle was camped in a rocky hollow, with natural ramparts all around!

But they were scared men or they would not have been sitting so quietly and warily in that rocky basin!

Ben sat and took stock. Somewhere in that hollow was Tom. He had to be got out. That was the job.

Ben backed away. The posse had to be brought up silently, and then three determined men had to try getting into that basin without making a sound!

9

Hellion's Holocaust

BEN finished telling the men what he had found, and when Bantley and Bainter rode in a few seconds later, they came out with the same news.

"Wal, it checks," said Ben with a chuckle. "Let's git going. When we hit the lava bed, leave the hosses, men. Don't fancy takin' hosses across that rock. We approach on foot, an' then wait for it. Jack and Hoot are going with me into the basin—if we git in. Shore hope we do. We want to git Tom Wilson out somehow so that Stangle got no hold on us. Then we let blaze—unless Stangle's willin' to quit."

"He'll not do that," said a voice with conviction.

"Nope. It's a necktie party for him, anyway. All right. Everyone got it pat?"

The low growls that were uttered were all assenting!

The posse went silently forward with just the

182

soft slush of hoofs in sand. The men were ready and gun-itchy!

Ben judged their progress by the jagged walls of the canyon which reared up on their left. Soon the flat bed of rock was reached and the party dismounted. There was some activity while the men hobbled their horses. They did not want them to take fright at any gun-fire and shy off into the desert bed of the canyon.

Eventually the party moved forward on foot. Most of the riders had wrapped strips of cloth round their spurs to prevent them jingling, and with hats pulled down low their faces were well shadowed.

The men went softly round the basin until it was surrounded, but they kept a good distance from the actual ramparts of the rocky fort Jed Stangle had chosen for a stand. The little sound they did make was muffled by the fair distance they kept from the basin. One or two men climbed the high wall of the canyon, taking Winchesters with them. If they could see anything, they would be able to shoot down into the basin. In the darkness they could shoot only at gun flashes, but that had not started yet. In this much, Jed Stangle had erred in choosing the basin, but even so, for men approaching along the canyon bed, he was in a strong position. And maybe he had figured the posse would blunder into his natural fort!

Then Ben beckoned to Hoot and Jack. They were going forward in an attempt to rescue Tom Wilson!

They slithered forward inch by inch on their stomachs, separating all the time. The basin in the canyon bed was pretty wide, to judge from the shadows that occasionally moved, and they wanted to approach from different angles.

Ben Harvey eventually found himself alone in the dark. He ceased his snake-like progress for a few seconds and listened intently. He was wondering if he could hear Hoot and Jack as they moved slowly to the basin, but the hot night seemed to muffle all sounds. He crept on again, realising that the last few yards might be dangerous. Anyway the whole thing inevitably had plenty of risk. Someone might see Jack or Hoot and raise the alarm—it was all very chancy, but the risks had to be taken.

Ben went on, taking the utmost pains over every little movement of his body and hugging the flat earth. In this way he reached the rough parapet that surrounded the rocky basin, and he saw that the fort Stangle had chosen was bigger than he had thought. The owl-hoots were not numerous enough to be everywhere, and Ben had luckily approached a spot which was unguarded.

He crawled to the jagged perimeter, wondering where Hoot and Jack had reached, and then suddenly threw himself into the basin in a slithering headfirst motion.

Almost immediately he saw a group of horses standing like dark shadows near a rocky upthrust. Stangle's remuda, he thought. The outlaw was hanging on to those cayuses apparently thinking he would live to use them.

Within seconds he had reached the remuda, and he walked gently among the horses, making no sudden movement because he did not want to spook the animals. He walked round slowly, and soon his keen eyes noticed he was in the centre of the basin and that the shadowy figures of the outlaws were all around the perimeter now with their backs to him.

Apparently he had just got through at the right moment. Maybe Hoot and Jack were still outside the basin, seeking a chance to worm in.

And then he came across a pile of saddles and other gear. Experience told him this was the natural centre of Stangle's camp and that Tom Wilson could hardly be far away.

Ben stood behind a tall horse, a dim unseen figure, and surveyed the dark shadows. He could see the deeper bulk of the piled-up stores, but he could not make out the details.

He would have to get closer. He had to look somewhere for the old-timer. Until he was rescued the attack could not start.

He took three quiet steps to the heaps and then suddenly realised he was peering at a bound figure. In the gloom he had been unable to discover the nature of one heap from another, but this was Tom Wilson!

Quickly Ben went down beside the old fellow and whipped out a knife. There was no sound from Tom. Ben saw that he was gagged. Before he untied the gag, Ben whispered, "Don't make a sound, Tom. It's me—Ben Harvey!"

And then the sharp knife was slicing through the rope as if it was butter. Tom uttered a slight gasp of relief which he could hardly restrain, but it was the only sound. There was no need for words. He would follow Ben Harvey to freedom—or death!

Presently Tom was actually free of the bonds —but they still had to get out of the basin.

Ben handed him a Colt.

He whispered into Tom's ear, "Don't use it until yuh have to."

Tom Wilson nodded.

They moved silently into the group of horses. One horse snorted and turned, but there was little other noise. Ben and Tom tensed, wondering if the outlaws would look towards the remuda, but nothing happened. Evidently the horses were thought to be pretty quiet.

What would happen when the shooting started was anybody's guess.

Suddenly their progress towards the parapet of the basin was blocked by the shadowy figure of a man who sat behind a boulder staring out into the night.

The man had to be tackled. There was no way past him, for to edge more to the right or left meant getting too close to the other crouching outlaws.

Ben nudged Tom Wilson, and then left the old-timer almost hidden in a cleft. Ben moved softly up to the owl-hoot, taking it so stealthily that he even moved little stones to one side before he went forward.

He was now only feet away from the un-suspecting man, and Ben's lips were a tight, compressed line. He had a great urge to jump the man and get it over, but he knew he might make a noise. There had to be no noise—not yet.

And so he came to within inches and only then did the man move uneasily, as if conscious of some unknown thing. Ben leaped and the butt of his Colt came down on the man's hat, crushing through the flimsy protection and grinding on to the skull.

The outlaw rolled over with scarcely a groan.

Ben took away his gun and ammunition. There might be spare guns, but at least it was one less. He had thoughts of taking the man, too, but he abandoned the idea. The man would be out of any events for some time yet.

Tom had seen the man go over, for he came creeping up to Ben Harvey. Within seconds they were over the jagged perimeter and moving quickly outwards when suddenly Colts roared in the night!

The shots came from within the basin and not from the waiting posse hiding all around.

Ben jerked his head, halted a second.

It looked as though Hoot and Jack had run into trouble.

"Git runnin', Tom!" Ben muttered fiercely to the old-timer beside him.

They rose to their feet and ran like the wind. The darkness swallowed them and no bullets came their way. Within a few seconds they had run into a group of three possemen.

"Now yuh're safe," jerked Ben. "We can throw lead at those hombres. Shore hope Hoot and Jack can get out without stopping lead."

And as a signal he fired six shots into the air. Hoot and Jack would know that Tom was safe, and it was understood that they began to withdraw on hearing those six rapid shots.

The possemen still held their shooting. Until Jack and the sheriff returned they could not be sure of their targets.

The six signal shots roused some wild shooting from the outlaws in the basin. Flashes of red stabbed the air and Colts roared. But it was simply the shooting of desperate men firing at shadows and less.

Tom Wilson found his voice at last.

"Linda—did yuh git Linda away safe an' sound, son?"

"Shore did. Back on the ranch right now."

"Guess I owe yuh all the gold in them Guadalupes," cackled Tom.

Ben laughed as he peered into the shadows ahead.

"Did hear Hoot Bainter say somethin' about gold. Figure he wouldn't mind pickin' up some gold from those Guadalupes himself!"

"Guess that's an idea," retorted Tom. "Yes, sir. Maybe I gotta think that out. But gimme a gun right now."

"Yuh got my colt."

"Shore, an' yuh can have it back. I want a rifle. Got any?"

"Yeah. But yuh better stay back here. Yuh've seen enough trouble for the time being, old-timer."

"Trouble, nuthin'!" rapped Tom Wilson. "I aim to git one o' two o' them hellions for what they done to me. Why they jest 'bout tried to kill me, the varmins. Wanted my gold. They'll never see gold," concluded Tom definitely, and he spat into the darkness.

There was a low laugh all round.

"Give the old firebrand a rifle," said Ben. "He—"

An interruption came. Two men lurched out of the gloom, one holding his shoulder. The three possemen held them and steadied them.

"Those hombres started shootin' at us!" gasped Hoot Bainter indignantly.

"We never got past the outside rim o' that basin," jerked Jack Bantley ruefully. "Those fellers were sittin' all around. Then we heard yore shots. Got Tom away? Good for yuh, Ben!"

"All right. We'll give those owl-hoots a taste o' lead," shouted Ben Harvey.

Then flame lanced the darkness all around as the possemen began to advance to closer range. Colts roared and Winchesters barked. The owl-hoots answered back at once with a hail of wildly fired bullets.

Ben Harvey knew that this attack would be a long affair. The outlaws were sitting pretty good behind that jagged parapet. They might last until morning easily, because aiming at gun flashes was an erratic business. For one thing a good marksman moved a bit after every shot, knowing full well that the return fire would seek his last spot.

Ben judged the possemen were all around the basin in good advantage points. It would not pay to get too close. This was a game where they had to be satisfied if they could pick off a few outlaws slowly and with great expenditure of slugs.

And so it proved. Ben got behind a good rock with plenty of jagged clefts through which to poke a gun. As it was dark, he could show himself pretty freely—though the outlaws could not see him, naturally. They answered his gun flashes though. A number of slugs pinged on the rock, sending up spurts of chips and dust.

The attack settled down. The possemen shot only when a gunflash jagged out of the dark basin or when they saw an occasional dark shadow move against the lighter tones of the background. The owl-hoots promptly returned lead, using Colts and rifles.

The desperadoes behind the basin realised this was a last stand. By sunup they would be in a worsening position. True they might be able to make a break, but it was a risky game. Rifles could pick off any fleeing horseman. After the sun came up, it would become terribly hot in the rocky basin—though the same applied to the possemen.

Ben tried the effect of a call to surrender.

"Stangle—can yuh hear me? Are yuh there?"

There was silence and then a voice snarled: "I kin hear yuh. What yuh want?"

"I ask yuh to surrender, in the name of the Texas Rangers."

"Yuh kin go to hell!"

Ben laughed grimly, and did not attempt another call. Jed Stangle meant his words, there was no doubt about that.

The next hour dragged with a fitful burst of lead slinging and an involuntary shout of pain from the basin. It was not the first curse that Ben had heard during the night—and on both sides, admittedly. He had carefully made a check on each such shout, trying to estimate the casualties Stangle's gang had suffered.

The purple haze on the horizon lightened, showing the landscape a great deal more clearly. Now it was essential to keep under cover. On both sides the men were aiming at definite targets and not just at gun flashes. It was getting lighter every minute.

"Won't be long now," muttered Ben.

On his right Hoot Bainter crouched behind a rock similar to Ben's.

"Guess those hombres ain't too happy now!" bawled the sheriff. "They'll make a break—jest yuh watch."

Either way it was death to the owl-hoots and they knew it. The sun seemed to rise suddenly, with its usual habit in these parts, and the heat rose steadily.

All at once there was movement among the bunched horses in the basin. A few of the animals had stopped bullets and were dead, but the rest had been tightly roped together during the night.

Now all at once, with the coming of the sun, the rope corral seemed to burst and badly scared horses stampeded in a mad bunch towards the far end of the basin.

And a number of the horses were saddled and carrying riders literally flattened along the animals' necks. Unseen the outlaws had crept among the remuda, got their horses and were now riding out in a desperate bid for freedom.

But before the first horses jumped the parapet, marksmen had picked off two men. They fell forcefully to their death amid pounding hoofs.

Ben was standing, aiming at Jed Stangle. He could see the outlaw chief's dusty back lying low on a big mare. Even as Ben aimed and fired, the outlaw swung over the side in Indian fashion. Ben's bullet just did not get him.

And then the outlaws were out of the basin and digging steel into the horses. Two more rolled off before a few yards were traversed with pounding hoofs. Five seemed to be getting away when the Winchesters barked again, and two owlhoots fell to rocky terrain and lay still.

Ben shoved his guns back into his holsters. He ran with every ounce of his strength to the basin where a badly spooked horse had broken away from the stampeding remuda and was turning back. It was galloping straight to Ben!

Ben knew there was not much time. His own horse and the rest of the possemen's mounts were corraled well back from the basin.

He came up to the saddleless horse and, grasping the mane, swung himself to its back. The horse crow-hopped and Ben hung on, arms round its neck. Then he got it under control and wheeled it round. He fed it steel and drove it after the outlaws.

By the time the possemen got to their horses, Ben was well ahead, going grimly after the three desperate outlaws who had survived the battle.

He was gaining, too. The horse he was riding had evidently not borne a rider the previous day and was quite fresh. Ben was gaining on the three fleeing men.

They were swinging down the wide sandy

waste of the canyon bed. There were few obstructions. It was a ride to the finish.

An outlaw drew a gun, twisted in the saddle and fired. The slug went wide. Ben grinned.

"The range is right, feller," he muttered, "but yuh can't shoot. How's about this?"

He got his Colt, steadied and squeezed the trigger twice. The man ahead rolled slowly over the side of his horse. His leg tangled with the reins, and the cayuse pulled him along the sandy bed for some yards in a cloud of dust.

Ben fired again, coolly. He missed once, twice—then the third bullet got a target. The man dived to the earth as the heavy slug spun him off his saddle.

But Ben had slowed his horse somewhat to concentrate on his shooting, and Jed Stangle's cayuse had increased its lead.

Ben lay flat along his horse's neck and fed it steel. Riding without a saddle was not new to him—it was part of his training in the Rangers.

He was getting near to Stangle when the other twisted and fired a wild, wide shot. But Stangle saw how near Ben was and that it was always an advantage to the pursuer to be able to shoot without twisting. He knew death was on his heels, and all at once he leaped from his horse at full speed and jumped behind a big rock—boots slithering into cover amid a shower of dust and dirt.

Ben halted his horse as Stangle blazed away with his guns. Slugs tugged his hat into the air. Then Ben rode back out of range.

He rode round the man, still out of range, and Stangle slithered desperately to the cover side of his rock.

"The posse will be up, Stangle," shouted Ben. "Yuh're trapped. They'll get all around yuh. A rifle can pick yuh off. Yuh're finished. All I gotta do is wait."

"Yuh yellow-bellied—" bawled Stangle.

There was venom in his voice even though he had to shout to make himself heard.

"I'll give yuh a chance, Stangle," said Ben, slowly. "Come out o' that rock. Yuh can start shootin' when yuh think yuh in range. I'll do same. That gives yuh a chance."

And Jed Stangle knew it. He came out immediately.

Sheer hate was twisting his face. All he could think of was the chance to kill the man who had foiled him.

Ben jumped down from the horse. He strode

out, hands near his gun-belt, his eyes on Stangle.

Jed Stangle came on, a shambling figure caked in dust. Oaths fell from his lips, and his eyes glittered with a strange fury.

He got in range and both men suddenly whipped guns out and fired simultaneously.

Ben felt red-hot pain sear across his ribs. One hand went to his side and felt the blood already spurting through his shirt.

Jed Stangle halted abruptly and spun round. He fell to the earth, but he gripped his gun all the time. As he sat, with disbelief all over his face, his mind seemed to clear.

He deliberately raised his gun and fired at Ben. The bullet went wide, but Ben, not anticipating that, fired at the same time.

His bullet slammed Stangle backward, head bouncing against the ground. He managed to roll over on his face and push himself up on to his knees. He slowly turned round. His muscles convulsed in a fruitless effort to pull the trigger and his eyes widened with the horrible realisation that death was upon him. His head sank and his knees buckled. He fell on his face and did not move.

Ben stared for a second and turned,

muttering. The sun beat down like a red orb on the silent desert.

Ben got to his horse but could not mount. Stangle's bullet had passed along his side, just outside the ribs. It would heal, but right now he felt oddly weak.

And then the posse came thundering up. They saw the dead outlaw chief and Ben as he lurched against his horse.

"Doggone me, if yuh ain't catched a bullet!" roared Hoot Bainter. "Hyar, git up on my hoss!"

And he got down and helped Ben Harvey up to the saddle. Then he climbed up and the whole party turned back.

Vultures wheeled in the sky, scenting the death in the canyon.

Old Tom Wilson was plenty concerned at Ben's wound.

"Yuh know what—I'm agoin' to raise a party to git some more gold out them Guadalupes an' share it out among the gents that got me away from that hellion," he said. "Yes, sir! Plenty o' gold for all in them hills!"

"Are yuh agoin' with the party, Tom?" queried one man.

There was a roar of laughter when Tom

cackled, "No, sir! I'm an oldster now. Let them young 'uns git the gold. I'll tell 'em where to look. Ain't that good enough?"

"Why were yuh so plumb anxious to keep Stangle and his owlhoots away from the gold, Tom?" asked Hoot Bainter.

"Hellions like that don't know how to use good wealth," said Tom, slowly. "I'd 'ave died afore I'd let them git it!"

Ben Harvey grinned back at the old-timer.

"Wal, Stangle got his."

Somehow he felt it was a relief that his mission was over.

Now to get back to Toughgrass and behave like a gentleman!

Other men had wounds, and as they were being attended to Ben's thoughts turned to pictures of Linda.

Yes, sir! He had to get back to town and show that girl he could behave like a real fine fellow.

Because he was sure she expected it!

BRETT RANDALL, GAMBLER
by E. B. Mann

Larry Day had the choice of running away from the law or of assuming a dead man's place. No matter what he decided he was bound to end up dead.

THE GUNSHARP
by William R. Cox

The Eggerleys weren't very smart. They trained their sights on Will Carney and Arizona's biggest blood bath began.

THE DEPUTY OF SAN RIANO
by Lawrence A. Keating and
Al. P. Nelson

When a man fell dead from his horse, Ed Grant was spotted riding away from the scene. The deputy sheriff rode out after him and came up against everything from gunfire to dynamite.

SUNDANCE: IRON MEN
by Peter McCurtin

Sundance, assigned to save the railroad from a murder spree, soon came to realise that he'd have to fight fire with fire, bullets with bullets and death with death!